Touch of Phenomenon

Touch of Phenomenon

AVIS DILLON

LitPrime Solutions
21250 Hawthorne Blvd
Suite 500, Torrance, CA 90503
www.litprime.com
Phone: 1-800-981-9893

Published by LitPrime Solutions   05/26/2022

ISBN: 979-8-88703-004-3(sc)
ISBN: 979-8-88703-005-0(e)

Library of Congress Control Number: 2022909073

Contents

Prologue

Every once in a while things happen in our lives that cannot be explained. We either come up with bizarre explanations, or try to ignore the incidents, especially if we do not want to believe in phenomena. Yet it is a fact of life, and it happens, and it can't always be explained by logical thinking.

This is a collection of fourteen short stories that leave us with a sense of wonder, a thought that maybe…just maybe…there are some things we simply have to accept. They may not be so pronounced as to be labeled "miracles," but nevertheless, we cannot use logic or scientific fact to explain them away.

Fantasy, you say? Perhaps.
Or perhaps not…

At The Waterfall

Jenna knelt down and dangled her fingers in the pool. The water was cold, but would be refreshing. Around her the light summer breeze gently moved the leaves of the oak tree. The songs of the birds were almost drowned out by the roar of the waterfall. Jenna spent a lot of time at the waterfall. In the winter, when weather allowed and the waterfall was not as profuse, she could slide behind the falls through a small opening between the rock and the water over a narrow ledge. In summer, the quickest way was simply to swim across the pond and hoist herself up under the falls onto the floor of the cave. Today was nearly 100 degrees, and definitely "swim weather."

Quickly she shed her jeans, boots and shirt, adjusted her bikini, and jumped directly into the water. Jenna was not a toe-dipper, and she shivered slightly, taking a deep breath as her face broke the surface. With slow even strokes she navigated to the center of the large pool, then swam toward the veil of shimmering water that spilled from the top of the ridge. Ducking under the waterfall, she hoisted herself up on the ledge of the shallow cave. It was cool and dim and provided some relief from the heat of the hot summer sun.

Jenna wanted to escape from more than the blazing sun. The situation back at the ranch was very uncomfortable. Her parents were constantly arguing and her brother was certainly not helping. He was using the constrained relationship to further his own interests, as he always did. Jenna and her older brother Ralph had conflicts as far back as she could remember. She had been looking forward to September, when she would be going to college in the next state.

Ralph had even sneered at her class schedule. Her driving interest was in American history, and he never tired of making fun of her career choice, calling it "dull," "boring" and "worthless." Jenna learned to tune him out years ago. She put a lot of it down to jealousy, as he barely managed to finish high school and had neither the ambition nor the intelligence to get into college. As far as she could see, his main interests were fast cars and fast girls. Their parents would probably be supporting him for the rest of his life… if he had his way. Mother catered to him and made excuses for his lack of ambition and failure to keep a job. Her father was about to wash his hands of the whole situation, which he wasn't happy with …thus the constant arguing.

This morning, however, was the final straw. Her parents reluctantly informed her that she wouldn't be going to college after all. Her college fund left to her by her grandfather --which she believed was secure -- was nearly gone...the money having been spent to bail Ralph out of a mess, preventing a law-suit and most likely jail time for the reckless young man. They had to make a choice, she was told, and her education was not as important as preventing Ralph from having a police record. There was a grand total of $1,000 left, which her mother suggested would gain her entrance to a secretarial course in a nearby town.

She twisted her long blonde hair to squeeze out as much water as possible and then slid over to lean against the side of the cave wall, settling into a more comfortable position. The gentle roar of the falling water was soothing and she closed her eyes, feeling more relaxed and clear-headed than she had for a long time.

Jenna stayed under the waterfall for over an hour, trying to decide on a course of action. She certainly couldn't stay at the ranch any longer. She couldn't afford to pursue her dream, which did not include being a secretary. Where her life was going to go from here, she had no idea.

Finally, she slipped back into the water, ducked under the waterfall and headed for shore.

As soon as she pulled herself from the water, she realized there was a problem...a serious problem. First of all, the weather had changed drastically and it was considerably colder than when she first arrived. Second, her clothes were not where she left them. Muttering curses under her breath and laying the blame on her brother, she looked around the area. A glimpse of cloth caught her eye on a small tree several feet from the bank and she pushed through the bushes.

The clothes were not hers. There was a faded cotton dress, white socks and a pair of shoes, along with a blanket and small towel, and a heavy jacket. No one else was around, and she really had no choice. Drying herself off with the towel and blanket as best she could, Jenna took off her wet bikini, and slipped on the dress, pulling on the socks in order to get her damp feet into the shoes. When she stood up, she was surprised to find the dress and shoes actually fit. Ralph really outdid himself this time. His practical jokes usually weren't so elaborate, and at least he had added a jacket since the temperature had unexpectedly dropped.

She picked her way back up the path, feeling a bit uneasy but not sure why, except things seemed slightly unfamiliar. The trees and brush didn't look quite right. When she reached the fence...or where the fence should be...there was nothing but a meadow of brown stubble. Perplexed, she continued on the path through the field. The barn should have been just on the other side, but there was nothing but more woods. She had lived in this area all her life and knew it like the back of her hand, but suddenly everything was totally different. It was impossible and...frightening.

Confused and disorientated, Jenna stood at the entrance to the woods, not knowing where to turn. This was her father's land. What happened to the ranch...the barn...the fence? Not knowing what else to do, she continued up the path through the copse of woods.

In the next clearing she saw the house and breathed a sigh of relief until she realized that the house, familiar though it was, was also different. They had painted it last year, but now it desperately needed a coat of paint ...and the addition her father had added when he first took over the farm was missing. The house looked exactly like the pictures in the family's old album...just like it did when her grandparents owned it! The rickety barn sat to the side...where the barn used to be until her father had it torn down and replaced with the large solid building she expected to see on the other side of the meadow.

A tall, brown-haired woman came out from the kitchen door and stood on the porch, shading her eyes against the sun. "Jennifer," she called, "where have you been? The chickens are waiting for their grain. Come finish your chores and help me with dinner."

Aghast, Jenna recognized a younger version of her grandmother from the family album...her grandmother who had been gone for nearly fifty years! She rubbed her eyes and looked again. Nothing changed. The woman turned and entered the house again, and Jenna, not having any other options, went to the chicken coop and fed the flock. She had fed the chickens every day since she was a child, and the chicken coop was where it always was and looked basically the same. This at least was familiar, even if the dog following her, wagging his tail, wasn't. He seemed friendly enough and certainly didn't treat Jenna like a stranger.

Not knowing what else to do, she continued on to the house and entered the back door. The woman looked up, smiled, and handed her an apron, chatting about peeling the potatoes as she shoved more wood into an old-fashioned stove.

A time warp? Was that possible? Jenna could think of nothing else that would explain where she was. It was obviously not 2001 anymore. How and why she had been flung back to when her grandparents owned the land was outside of her comprehension, but unless she had hit her head while swimming and was unconscious and dreaming, she was in the same place but in some other time. She tried to calculate in her mind, based on her grandmother's appearance, what year it might be but the shock was making it difficult for her to even think. And who did her grandmother think *she* was? Vaguely she remembered her father mentioning that he once had an older sister named Jennifer... and something had happened to her before he was even born. Jenna strained to remember what he had said but hadn't really paid much attention at the time.

Dutifully she peeled the potatoes, wiped off the table and accepted the dishes the woman handed her to set the table. Four plates...no doubt her grandfather, grandmother and herself...and one other. Her father had an older brother, Thomas. Uncle Tommy and his family lived in California and visited usually once a year. A tall, boisterous hefty man with a shock of blonde hair burst in the door, followed by a young boy. Jenna's heart leaped as she realized this was her uncle Tommy. His age appeared to be about six. Tommy was seven years older than her father, who was born in 1942, so apparently her father had not even been born yet.

Supper was an interesting meal for Jenna. Tommy, continually being reminded not to talk with his mouth full, enthused over a baseball game at school. The bread was freshly baked, the meat tender and the cake light and fluffy, which was quite a feat, considering the oven her grandmother had to work with. When everyone left the table, Jenna quietly cleared the dishes, scraping the plates with the leftovers into a large dish on the counter automatically, although she wasn't sure why she did. Her grandmother took the dish outside and Jenna realized it was to feed the dog. It occurred to her that she must have tapped into at least part of Jennifer's psyche.

After the dishes were done...her grandmother washed and she dried... Jenna said goodnight and climbed the stairs, hoping she would know where Jennifer's room was.

The first door she opened, which she knew as her parent's room, was obviously her grandparent's, and the one next door seemed to be decorated for a young girl. Although it was not the same room she was used to, since she was the only girl in the family, this must be the place.

She spent the next half hour poking around the room, peering into the desk and dresser drawers and checking out the closet. A glance in the mirror confirmed that she looked the same as always, but she suspected that her new-found family didn't see her that way. Jenna's hair was blonde with lighter blonde highlights, long and straight. The only picture in the album that she remembered marked "Jennifer at 16" showed a young lady with much shorter hair and much darker than her own. Touching her hand to her head confirmed that her hair was not long as it appeared in the mirror to her eyes, but much shorter. She wondered how old she was supposed to be in this new life.

She retrieved her wet bikini from the pocket of her dress and hung it on a hook in the closet to dry. A long cotton nightgown in the dresser replaced her dress and she climbed into bed gratefully, extremely tired. Time travel was apparently exhausting, she thought, prepared to fall asleep and hopefully to wake up the next morning in her own bed in the right year.

Predawn was barely showing when Jenna awoke. The rooster's early morning wakeup call, soothing in its familiarity, announced the new day. It took several minutes for her to realize that she was still in Jennifer's room. Turning over in bed, she felt a lump under the other pillow, which turned out to be a book...actually a diary. Delighted, she came fully awake. Now maybe she could find some clues as to why she had taken over the life of a girl several decades ago. Not bothering to dress, she lit the kerosene lamp, sat cross-legged in the center of the bed and opened the diary.

The first entry was dated August fifth, with no year following. The author described her birthday celebration, one of the gifts being the diary. "It seems so strange to realize I am finally sixteen. I wish my parents would treat me like the adult I really am. They just don't seem to understand how I feel about Joseph. I've loved him for so many years, but Mother says I was just a child and couldn't have fallen in love, but I did. I've loved Joseph since we first met ten years ago, when I was five years old, but they just don't understand."

And an entry a few days later..." The news from the War in Europe is not good. Father fears that America will soon be involved. President Roosevelt and the Prime Minister of England signed something called the Atlantic Charter, and it pulls us closer and closer to the fighting in Europe. I am terrified that Joseph will join the army, as he has told me he wants to do as soon as he turns 21. "

Jenna realized immediately that this entry pinpointed the year as 1941. History being her favorite subject, she was very familiar with the years surrounding both World Wars. The Atlantic Charter, cornerstone to the United Nations, was signed around August 12, 1941, a few months before the Pearl Harbor attack. Although being thrown back to that era was causing her real panic, it was also rather exciting to be experiencing those events first hand. Quickly she flipped through the pages of writing to where the entries stopped about halfway to the end.

The last entry was dated December 4th: "Joseph met me by the waterfall this afternoon. He told me he is joining the army. He is not old enough to enlist, but he said several of his friends are lying and claiming they are 21 and he will do the same. I begged him not to do this. I just know that we are going to get involved in this horrible war and I fear for his life...and mine if I lose him. "

She decided that the December 4th date must be in 1941, since the Japanese attacked Pearl Harbor on the 7th. Being the last entry, she had to assume that Jennifer had written it within the day or two. No wonder it was so cold out! Knowing what year she had landed made her feel a little better, for some reason. Should she keep up the diary? She desperately wished she had paid more attention to her father when he was talking about his sister and what happened to her. Was she there to stop whatever was going to happen to Jennifer? Or would it happen to her? Would she ever get back to her own time? Maybe if she went back to the waterfall and under the falls....

"Jennifer," called a voice from the bottom of the stairs. "Are you awake?"

"Coming. Just let me get dressed," Jenna replied, wondering if she should call the woman downstairs "Mother." Hurriedly she washed her face in the basin and put on underwear from the dresser and a fresh dress from the closet.

No one seemed to notice that "Jennifer" was any different than they were used to. She helped her "mother" in the kitchen prepare breakfast and then went out to gather the eggs and feed the chickens...chores that were almost identical to those she had always performed at home. Tommy was at school, but apparently Jennifer did not attend.

Late in the afternoon she found herself alone and slipped back to the waterfall. Perhaps she could find her way back to her own time if she went back to the cave under the falls. Before she could slip through the opening and behind the falls, she heard someone coming. A young man rode into the clearing, jumped from the saddle and swept her up in a bear hug.

"Jenny, my love, I did it. I enlisted. Please don't be mad at me, sweetheart. I have to do this."

Jenna opened her mouth to tell him she was not his "Jennifer" but instead the words that she spoke were not what she intended. "But what will become of me…and the baby?" Jenna clamped her hand over her mouth. Had she said that…really? Baby? My Lord, was Jennifer *pregnant*? Maybe she should have read more of the diary!

"Come with me. I don't know when I will have to leave for training, but wherever it is, we'll be together unless I get sent overseas, and even if there is a war sometime in the future, it won't last long and then we can make a home for ourselves and our new baby. Have you told your parents yet?"

Jenna shook her head. She could safely assume that Jennifer had not revealed her condition in light of the normal, offhand way she was treated. No doubt there would have been a much different reception if it was known that she was pregnant.

"Jenny, I have a plan. Meet me here later tonight. The moon is still pretty full so it will be light enough to find your way. Everything will be alright. We'll be together and nothing can separate us, and I know exactly where we can go. My grandparents have a farm just outside Seattle. I'll just tell the Army that I am only 19 and not 21 and I know they will let me out. Just bring a few clothes. We can buy whatever you need when we arrive in Washington. I'll borrow my father's car and we can take the train from town. Someone will get the car back to him, I'm sure. We'll be happy, Jenny, love. I know we will."

Was this what happened to Jennifer then? Did she run away with her Joseph?

Suddenly Jenna had a horrible thought. "Joseph, what date is today?"

"December 6th, of course. Why?"

"And the year?"

Jennifer, what's the matter? You know it's 1941. Are you feeling alright?"

"War," she whispered. "By tomorrow night we'll be at war. There isn't enough time for us to go to Washington."

Joseph frowned and looked at her strangely. "I don't know what on earth makes you think so, but if that should happen, I promise I won't leave you. If they won't let me out, we'll still run away somewhere and I just won't go in the Army."

"It's too late," she cried. "You already joined. You can't desert. They'll put you in jail...maybe execute you!" Jenna was disturbed at herself for being upset. Why? She didn't even know this young man.

"Everything will be fine, Jenny." Joseph said soothingly as he wrapped his arms around her, pulling her close. "Just meet me here tonight. If I tell them I am not old enough, I'm sure they won't even want me. By the time we get involved with the War, if we ever do and if I have to go, you and I will already be in Washington and you can stay with my grandparents until it's over and I come home."

He kissed her quickly, jumped on the horse and disappeared through the trees.

Slowly Jenna walked back up the path, her plan to slip behind the falls forgotten for the moment. Back at the ranch, she quickly ran upstairs to her room and pulled out the diary, flipping it to the last page. Shocked, she looked at the page and realized it was a new entry... and she had not made it.

"December 6th," it read. "Joseph has joined the Army, but he said he will not leave me. He's going to tell them he isn't old enough so they will let him out. We have plans to meet tonight and run away together. I cannot tell my parents that I am pregnant. I know they would never forgive me. We will make a new life for ourselves far away and maybe someday they will let me come home to see them again."

So entries were still being made in the diary but not by Jenna. Quickly she tucked the diary in back under the pillow. She would have to hide it somewhere safe... somewhere she could locate it again after she returned to her own time...if she ever did. If the entries continued, perhaps she could find out what happened to Jennifer.

She thought about hiding the book in the barn, but then remembered that the barn was torn down by her father and rebuilt in another place. A search of the barn, however, did yield something she could use...a metal box and a large piece of oilskin. Wrapping the diary in a smaller piece of the oilskin, she put it inside the metal box, using the rest to wrap the box tightly. Did oilskin deteriorate over time? She didn't know, but it would protect the book from the water right now. Jenna had decided on the perfect hiding place...the cave inside the waterfall.

The sky was clouding up and a storm was brewing. She decided she would have to go early to the waterfall early and stash the box before Joseph arrived. She started for the house, but she was barely outside the barn when the sky opened up in a drenching, icy rain. She went back into the barn, hoping the deluge would become lighter, but when it started getting dark, she gave up hoping. Tucking the box under her arm, she ran for the house and burst through the back door.

"Goodness, child. You'll catch your death. Run up and change, honey," her grandmother directed. Jenna did as she was told, hoping the woman would not notice the box she carried. When she reached Jennifer's room, she hurriedly shoved her treasure under the bed and then stripped off her soaking wet clothes, drying her hair as best she could with the towel hanging by the washbasin.

The storm showed no signs of letting up. She helped with supper, listening to the conversations around the table without joining in. Apparently that was the way Jennifer usually behaved as it drew no comment from the others. She cleared the table, quietly washed and dried the dishes and put them away, all the while listening to the rain and wind, which seemed to be getting worse instead of better. Obviously there would be no meeting at the waterfall tonight.

It was dark by the time supper was over, and the rest of the family adjourned to the living room and the fireplace. Even though it was still early, she lit another lamp, wished everyone goodnight and climbed the stairs to her room. No one seemed surprised, so this must be a common practice with the real Jennifer.

Back in the room, she unwrapped the diary, intending to read more of the earlier entries. She checked the last page again, and there was another entry which had not been there before. It was added to the entry after the December 6th date: "A terrible storm has prevented us from meeting. I trust Joseph did not go to the waterfall and wait for me. Perhaps tomorrow will be better and if the rain stops, we can continue with our plans. I have a bag packed with some of my clothing, but cannot bring everything. I will, of course, be sure to bring my diary as I do not want my parents to learn about the impending child this way. I will write them from Washington when we arrive so they will not worry."

Jenna looked around the room. Just inside the closet door was a leather bag. Apparently Jennifer had, in fact, packed to leave. This was eerie...who was writing in the diary and packing a bag when Jenna was running around in Jennifer's body? Whoever heard of such a thing? She suddenly became desperate to travel back to her own time, but the raging storm outside was not about to let her get back to the waterfall cave, where she instinctively felt the "portal to the future" was.

Having nothing else to do, she pulled on the nightgown and crawled into bed. This was a perfect time to read the rest of the diary.

The entries covered a span of several months. Jennifer had received the diary as a gift on her birthday in August, and she wrote about her excitement over a new gown for her sixteenth birthday, events that happened on the farm, Tommy's birthday, trips into town, inter-dispersed with comments about the ever growing war in Europe. Many passages were dedicated to Joseph and how wonderful he was. A passage in October was written in such a way that Jenna assumed that a clandestine encounter in the barn was when the pregnancy occurred, so she calculated that Jennifer was, on that date in December 1941, about two months pregnant. A short bout of morning sickness, according to the diary, was explained away as a touch of the flu, and fortunately for the girl and her secret, the nausea passed quickly. Curious, Jenna pushed on her stomach but it didn't feel any different than it ever did.

It was rather late when Jenna finally blew out the lamp and snuggled down to sleep. The storm was still raging outside although sometimes it seemed to quiet down a bit for long periods of time. Still, the rain continued to beat on the roof and the wind frequently rattled the windows. Jenna didn't expect to fall asleep, but did so and spent a dreamless night.

The next two days were not much better. The rain continued to fall, although the wind had died down. It was far colder than Jenna liked and she suspected that it would not be safe to try to enter the cave because of the storm. The waterfall would be raging, and the small entranceway blocked by water. By afternoon the rain had stopped and the sun pushed its way through the lingering clouds. Jenna sloshed out to feed the chickens through the standing pools of water in the yard.

She didn't know what to do about Joseph. If she met him, he would expect her to leave. Then she remembered...yesterday Pearl Harbor was bombed, and today was the day that the United States would officially declare war. She remembered that when we became part of the War, the government instituted the draft and lowered the age limit to 18. Since Joseph had already enlisted, they would likely not let him back out and he might already be gone. If that was the case, then Jenna was even more curious about what happened to Jennifer. Well, she wasn't going to wait around to see. When the rushing water subsided by the pool, she would make the trip to the cave, hide the diary and then hope she could get back through the portal or whatever it was to her own time.

Not having a radio, her "parents" had not heard about the Pearl Harbor attack on the 7th or the President's speech on the 8th, so it was the next morning before a neighbor drove over to inform the family that war had been declared and the young men in the area who had previously joined the service all left on the train that morning. The neighbor, Jenna discovered, was Joseph's father and this confirmed that she should not expect that the young man would be meeting the girl he thought was his Jennifer any time soon. So....if Jennifer didn't run away with Joseph, what on earth happened to her? Jenna had checked the diary daily, but no further entries appeared. Since she didn't know exactly when Jennifer disappeared, she wasn't about to wait around any longer than she had to.

Joseph's father stayed for coffee and of course the conversation was centered around the war and what would happen to the young men who would be doing the fighting overseas. When he finally left, she did her chores, helped in the kitchen and then escaped to her room. Late that afternoon, she dug out her bikini, slipped on the dress, stocking, shoes and the same jacket she had found that first day, and set out for the pond, the oilskin wrapped box under her arm. She was hoping desperately that the waterfall would allow her to slip between the water and rock and enter the cave. Jenna was terribly afraid that it was her last chance to escape back to her own time. Her biggest fear was that perhaps she was actually trapped in 1941 and would suffer the same fate as her Aunt Jennifer.

Surprisingly, she was going to miss this place. She had experienced a tiny piece of history, learned a lot about her ancestors and, hopefully, could eventually give her father Hank and his brother Tommy some indication through the mysterious diary as to what happened to their sister.

Jenna quickly ran down the path, through the woods and across the meadow, stopping on the edge of the pool rather out of breath. Shivering in the cold air, she quickly shed her outer clothes, hung them on a small tree off the ground and slid into the gap between the water and the rocks, grasping the box with its precious cargo. It was wet and slippery, but she carefully edged her way around the rock and under waterfall, breathing a sigh of relief when her feet were firmly on the cave floor.

The cave was not very deep. Jenna had explored it once or twice as a child, but this time she had a mission. Carefully feeling her way inside the walls, she finally found a large loose rock which came out with a little coaxing. Using her hands and another sharp stone from the floor of the cave, she dug out the soft earth behind the opening until it was big enough. It took her almost half an hour to make the hole large enough to accommodate the box and allow the rock to fit back inside its notch. Wryly, she surveyed her two broken fingernails.

When the box was concealed, she stuck her arms into the falling water to rinse off the dirt and then settled herself against the wall of the cave as she had done previously, closed her eyes and waited...for what she wasn't sure, but she felt she would know when it happened.

It was soothing, comfortable, and surprisingly warm under the waterfall, and Jenna found herself dozing. She quickly jerked herself awake. Was it safe to go back outside? She checked the temperature of the falling water and realized it was much warmer than it had been earlier. Letting herself down over the ledge, she ducked under the sheet of water and swam for shore.

When she emerged, she breathed a sigh of relief. Her jeans, boots and shirt were right where she left them. She was back! Quickly dressing, she ran up the path, over the fence and past the barn. The house, with its new paint job and the addition her father had added years ago, sat in the middle of the flowers and bushes that her mother had so carefully planted and tended. How long had she been gone? Apparently not long, for her mother greeted her cheerfully when she entered the house. Now the question was...could she retrieve the diary without being thrown back to 1941?

Ralph wasn't home for supper that night, for which Jenna was grateful. She wanted to talk to her parents without his interference.

"Dad," she asked casually, reaching for the bread, "you once told me you had a sister Jennifer but I don't remember what you said happened to her."

"Don't know," her father replied. "Nobody ever knew. She just up and disappeared one day. They think she might have drowned in the river but they never found a body. She spent a lot of time at the pond by the waterfall, I guess. I wasn't even born at the time and Tommy was just a little kid. "

"When did she disappear, do you remember?" Jenna asked, practically holding her breath for the answer.

"Let's see now. It was right after the War started. I remember Dad said there was some kind of scandal because the neighbor boy deserted the army a few days before so it must have been sometime in early or mid-December of '41 'cause it was about that same time, according to my parents. There had been a rainstorm a few days before and someone thought she probably fell into the river and was swept downstream, maybe as far as into the ocean."

Jenna wasn't surprised at his lack of emotion. After all, to him it happened to someone he never met and was decades in the past. To Jenna, it was only a few hours ago.

"Sure did tear up my parents, though. Tommy said things were never the same after she disappeared. Your grandma died a few years after having me, but Tommy always thought she really died of a broken heart."

Jenna helped her mother clear the table and then escaped upstairs. The room she knew as Jennifer's was now the guest room, and Jenna's was down the hall. As she gathered her laundry together, she couldn't help but wonder if Jennifer's disappearance coincided with her own return to her present life. She also wondered if the diary would be there when she returned to the cave. Jennifer wrote that she was going to take the diary with her when she left to spare her parents finding out she was pregnant. So much about this time travel thing was a mystery...there was no one she could actually go to about it without finding herself ensconced on a psychiatrist's couch somewhere. Well, she sighed, all she could do was try to retrieve the diary. If Jennifer's entries continued after Jenna left, there should be some clue as to where she disappeared to and why.

In the meantime, Jenna had to decide what to do with the rest of her life. Nothing had changed as far as college went. She still had no money to go. But she needed to get the remainder of her grandmother's trust fund and leave before Ralph found some other way to spend it.

Her parents drove into town the next afternoon to take Ralph to his court date. Jenna declined to go along. This was her chance to try to retrieve the diary. She changed into a swim suit, grabbed a towel and a garden trowel and headed for the waterfall, marveling at the fact that her trip to the past, which had lasted several days, was barely an hour of time in her world. She supposed there was a reason why she was thrown back to December 1941 when it was really July 2001 in her world.

It only took a few minutes using the trowel she had brought to loosen the stone and pull it from its nest. Yes, the box was there, and didn't look any worse for the wear. The oilskin had stood up very well over the years. Not waiting around to see if she was going to slip back into the past again, Jenna ducked under the sheet of water and headed for shore. She breathed a sigh of relief when she saw her towel right where she left it. Up the path, over the fence and around the barn and she was inside the house in less than ten minutes. Upstairs in her room she opened the box carefully and removed the diary.

Smiling, she saw there were two more entries after the last one she had read.

"December 9th: Joseph's father came by to tell us about the Japanese bombing Pearl Harbor and said that the President declared war yesterday. He said that all the young men in the neighborhood were on their way to training. Now it's too late. My Joseph is with the rest of them. I don't know what to do. By January it will be obvious that I am having a baby, and then perhaps my parents will send me away. I'm sorry to disappoint them both, but I cannot give up my baby. It's my only link to Joseph, and when he comes back from the war, we will be a complete family. I pray he comes back from this terrible war."

"December 10th: A miracle has happened. I went to the waterfall to see if the storm had made it too dangerous to enter the cave, and my Joseph came to me. They refused let him leave the Army, but he did not go with the rest of the young men after all. He left as they waited for the train to take them to camp and hid in the woods. I came back to the house to get my valise so we could run away together. I am going to leave this diary in the cave by the waterfall. Since Joseph has deserted, we must somehow find a safe place where he will not be caught. Washington is out of the question now. I think we must try to make it to Canada and hide there. Joseph was able to get some false documents to change our names. We will be known as Joseph and Jennifer Chase from now on and the papers show that we are citizens of Canada."

So…it seems that Joseph was one of the first protesters that went to Canada to avoid going into the service. Interesting! Apparently, Jenna mused, the clothes she left behind at the waterfall when she hid the box, convinced everyone that Jennifer drowned, and no one realized that more of her clothes were missing. Jenna still could not resolve her interaction with Jennifer, how Jennifer thought she hid the box and a few other details, but they would probably remain a mystery. This explained why the girl had never contacted her parents--Joseph was a deserter and they couldn't afford to be found.

Ah, but modern technology might take care of that problem. She changed into dry clothing and then booted up her computer and started a search for Joseph and Jennifer Chase in Canada. If they were still alive, she just might be able to find her father's missing sister.

It took quite some time, but she finally had a hit. Except it wasn't in Canada, it was in a little town on the outskirts of Seattle, Washington. Remembering what Joseph said about his grandparents having a farm near there, she decided to pursue the lead. She called the phone number, taking into consideration the three hour time difference.

"Hello, this is Jennifer," said the voice on the line.

"Hello. I'm sorry to disturb you, but I am looking for Jennifer Clark, formerly Jennifer Cole of Oxford, Georgia." Dead silence greeted her announcement for a moment.

"Who are you? What do you want?"

"Please don't hang up. My name is Jenna Cole. I'm her...your niece. I just want to connect you with your family again. My father was born after you left home, but your brother Tommy lives in California with his family..."

"Oh, my. Oh, my. Yes, yes, this is Jennifer Clark...Cole. How on earth did you find me?"

"It's a long story, and your diary is involved. For right now, let's just say that computers are wonderful things. May I tell your brothers where you are?"

"Oh, my, of course you can. But I'm not...it isn't...Well, I guess it's time we met and brought everything out in the open."

And so it was that Jennifer Cole Clark, who was well into her seventies, flew back to her old home in Georgia. Jenna could see the reflection of a youthful Jennifer when they met, and there was a surprising resemblance between her and her aunt.

There were a few awkward moments when she first arrived, but her obvious joy at being back at the old homestead soon had everyone at ease. Carol and Hank, Jenna's parents, greeted her with enthusiasm and a loving welcome. There was barely time to drop Jennifer's suitcase in her room and give her a quick tour outside before while Carol made dinner.

After eating, they settled into the living room with a cup of coffee... except Ralph, who was clearly uncomfortable and left as soon as he possibly could, making it known that he wanted nothing to do with this new intruder.

"It's time you all knew the real story here," began Jennifer, nervously turning her teacup around in the saucer. "And please don't pass judgment on anyone until I finish," she pleaded.

"The War started before Joseph had time to tell them he was too young, and once it did, it would not have done any good since they were dropping the age limit. Even though he had joined up, Joseph decided not to go into the service because I was expecting our child, and he refused to go overseas and leave me alone, so he became a deserter...a criminal...for my sake. I was barely sixteen and I knew my parents would have to send me away and force me to give up my child. The shame would be too great and they could not let me keep the baby."

Jennifer sat the teacup on the coffee table as she continued. "We made it to Canada somehow. Joseph had a distant relative way out in the country there who took us in. It was winter and bitter cold and we didn't have the clothing for it but they were very good to us. Joseph worked on their farm to pay our way. Because he was a deserter, we couldn't let anyone know where we were. By early spring things were getting better. The baby was due in July and I was feeling fine, but then Joseph came down with what we thought was just the flu. He was very sick, but he was afraid to see a doctor.

"I didn't know what to do, and I called my mother. She was so shocked and she told me everyone thought I had drowned. When I told her I was pregnant and Joseph was so ill, she immediately took a train to Canada. She wouldn't let me near Joseph as she was afraid I would catch whatever he had and lose the baby. She took care of him herself for almost four months but he never got better. He was still very ill when I had the baby. I begged her to take my son home with her to Georgia while I nursed Joseph back to health. She finally agreed."

There was a stunned silence when she finished. Jenna's father Hank was the first to realize what she was saying.

"Then ...then...are you saying you're...really my mother, and the woman I thought was my mother was ...my grandmother?" he asked quietly. Despite his calm voice, his face had lost most of its color. "Who else knew? Did Tommy? My father...er... grandfather?"

"Of course my father knew," Jennifer acknowledged softly. "I don't think Tommy did...he was so young, and Mother kept it from the neighbors. At first she avoided telling the neighbors anything because I had planned to come for you very soon...as soon as Joseph recovered. Later on, everyone was told that she had been pregnant when she took the trip--supposedly to visit relatives—so they weren't surprised that she returned with a baby. Remember, it was war time and a new baby for a neighbor was not exactly top priority for anyone to focus on."

"But why didn't you ever contact us? "Hank asked. "Why didn't you come and get me?"

"Joseph lingered for almost two months before he went into a coma. He lived nearly two years like that, and I took care of him every day. I finally called in a doctor, but they never did find out what was wrong with him. By the time he passed away, I couldn't suddenly show up in Oxford and announce that the toddler they had accepted as my parent's child was really mine. Everyone thought I was dead. I couldn't do that to my parents. They had helped me protect Joseph. Remember, he had been wanted by the government for desertion. At that point, I had no means of taking care of you anyway. You were better off where you were."

"Don't get me wrong," Hank hastened to say. "I had a wonderful childhood and my parents...grandparents were the greatest. It just feels strange to realize that what I believed all these years was...not true. It's going to take a while for this to sink in."

"After Joseph died, Joseph's grandparents asked me to come to Seattle and stay with them," Jennifer explained. "I had nowhere else to go and was there for over a year when the War finally ended. I helped his grandfather in their business for the next few years and when they passed away, they left me everything. Joseph's father, your neighbor, had passed away earlier in 1943 and there were no other heirs. He knew the truth, but I didn't know how much anyone else knew, and I certainly did not want to turn your lives upside down by intruding. I made my Will years ago leaving everything to my only son. Sooner or later, you would have known the true story, but I'm just as glad you discovered it before I left this earth."

The emotions of the evening left everyone exhausted, especially their elderly guest who had flown across the country. Jenna soon had her tucked up in the guest room, which used to be her old room, although it had changed considerably.

"This has been quite a revelation for our family," Jenna said, "Learning that I'm not your niece, I'm your granddaughter! My father especially will have to get used to knowing you are his mother."

"You never did tell me how you found me, Jenna. How did you find the diary and discover my new name?"

"You won't believe it when I tell you," Jenna replied. "Let's just say for tonight that our connection is a lot closer than you could even imagine. It's a long story and I'll tell you tomorrow when we visit the waterfall where this all began."

"There's one thing I want to do for you, my dear child. I'd like you to come to Seattle ...maybe attend to college out there. I can afford to give you a great education. I'm actually quite wealthy and have no one else to spend my money on. Joseph would have wanted me to do this, I'm sure. I wish you could have met him, Jenna."

"Oh, Grandmother..."

'I can make things much better for all of you now. I have so much to make up for."

"You have nothing to make up for. We are all just so happy to have you in our lives," Jenna protested, tears in her eyes.

"All except your brother," the older lady said wryly.

"Don't worry about Ralph. Dad rescued him from the consequences of his actions for the last time and convinced him to join the Army. Maybe they can straighten him out. And," she added, giggling, "he doesn't ever need to know about our grandfather ...I'm afraid that might give him ideas. He needs the discipline that going into the service will provide."

Jennifer sighed as she settled herself in bed. They would go to the waterfall tomorrow, and Jenna would tell her how she found the diary. For the first time since she lost Joseph, Jennifer had something in life to look forward to, and had her family back.

As for Jenna, she finally knew why she was sent back to 1941... it was her task to find her grandmother and settle a sixty-year-old mystery. Ralph might think history was dull, boring and worthless, but it certainly wasn't to the rest of the family!

The Earl's Daughter

The old-fashioned clock on the wall solemnly toned out the hour of midnight. Through the half-closed drapes, a dim light filtered in and outlined the dark shapes of the furniture…a large desk, one chair, a long sofa, and a curio cabinet in the corner. Two walls in the room were covered with bookshelves, floor to ceiling, and packed with books of all sizes and shapes. One wall was almost completely taken up with French doors opening onto the small stone patio. The fourth wall bore a huge fireplace, which was cold and full of ashes.

Outside, the snow-covered grounds and street beyond reflected the moonlight more than the dim streetlamp on the corner. Bushes and trees, bare from the winter, cast odd-shaped shadows on the ground. It was quiet, deadly quiet, and very still. No breeze, no passing traffic, no movement of animal or man. It was like the whole world was holding its breath.

The silence was broken by the clip-clop of horse's hooves as a small carriage turned up the long driveway. It stopped several yards away from the front door set back inside tall smooth white pillars. A lone figure slipped from the carriage door with a small valise and moved quietly across the snow-covered lawn to the French doors opening into the library. The carriage moved off around the circular driveway and back out into the street.

The French doors were opened just enough to allow the slight figure to slip inside. She sat the valise on the desk, threw off her long black cape and dropped it on the chair before pulling the drapes completely closed. With movements born of familiarity, she located a lamp and matches and soon the library became more welcoming.

With a small sigh, Marianne brushed her hand over her long red curls. If only she could just mount the stairs outside the library door and retire to her old room on the second floor. Only her room was empty of furnishings, its floor stripped of the pretty blue and yellow pile rug, the bed torn down and stored. Almost nothing in the house was the same as it was a few weeks ago…before her father disappeared. This library was the only room that remained as it had always been…furniture and books intact. No one seemed inclined to touch his personal papers as yet.

Marianne had been quietly and secretly living in that room for the last month, leaving only to do research at the library and find food to sustain herself. She could not start a fire in the fireplace, nor use the cook stove in the kitchen as she did not want anyone to realize that she was there. Fortunately, it was a rather mild winter and, despite the snow, it was only chilly and not bitingly cold outside. The house was solidly built and did not lose heat easily, as long as the flue on the fireplace was shut.

She had hidden a pillow and blanket in the bottom of the curio cabinet, and also using her cape, she made a bed on the sofa. As she was barely five feet tall, it was not cramped and she was rather quite comfortable.

Although she was very tired, more from the situation than anything else, she sat at the desk and continued her nightly ritual of sifting through every sheet and scrap of paper, not knowing exactly what she was looking for, but sure she would know when she found it.

Her father was not a very well-organized man, and Marianne found receipts from three years ago mixed in with letters from last month and lists of supplies which were undated with some crossed out and some not. It was a tremendous job to sort out and organize the contents of the desk and she was barely half through with the job. Surely somewhere there was a clue as to what happened to her father…where he was… why he disappeared without a trace.

There had been quite an outcry when the earl disappeared, taking with him, the world presumed, his only daughter. Marianne was not known in society, as she preferred the country and had spurned the social world after the first Season of her coming out. She had been bored, was not considered a "diamond of the first water" mainly due to her red hair and freckled completion, which was far from the rage. Her sponsor, an old friend of the family, was disgusted with her appearance and unable to bleach the freckles or tame the curly flaming locks.

After a very disappointing and somewhat insulting season, Marianne begged her father to send her to the country estate, where she had resided happily for the past three years, apparently forgotten by the ton of society. Happily, that is, until she had a dream that her father needed her, that he was hurt and was calling to her. Also in the dream, he kept pounding his fist on his desk, saying over and over "look here."

At first she simply blamed the fish she had for dinner the night before, but after three nights running of the same dream, she could no longer ignore the message. She immediately returned to London to the cottage of her old nurse, not wanting to announce to anyone else that she was there and learned that her father in fact had left on a journey but never reached his destination.

She had emptied the desk drawer and was running her hand inside to be sure she didn't miss any papers when she encountered a small lump. The light was too dim to be able to see what the tiny bump was…perhaps a spot of dried glue or some such thing…but as she pressed it, a panel on top of the desk slid open. A secret compartment! No one examining the construction of the desk would guess that the carved panel, matching the panel on either side, was anything but the decoration it appeared. Inside the opening was a packet of papers tied with a ribbon.

Her weariness forgotten, Marianne pulled out the papers to find a small packet of four letters, addressed to her father. The writing was faint and in the dim light of the lamp, she could only make out a few words. The first letter began "My dearest Tom" which caused Marianne to gasp. Marianne's mother had passed away some five years before, and to her knowledge, her father never sought other female company. In fact, he once said when she inquired if he wouldn't like to marry again, "I've had my soul mate, Mari. No one could ever take your mother's place."

She was torn between invading her father's privacy by reading his personal mail and wanting to know what the letters said. She convinced herself that the letters might hold the key to finding her father but needed better light to decipher them. She tucked them into her reticule to take with her to the public library the next morning. Pressing the tiny lump again closed the secret compartment, and Marianne took herself off to her sofa bed, blowing out the lamp and moving the drapes back to their original position.

Her dreams that night were disturbing. Again, she dreamed that her father was calling for her, and her deceased mother was there, reassuring her that no matter what happened, she loved her and always had.

The next morning, she awoke feeling surprisingly rested despite the turmoil of dreams during the night. Marianne stowed away her blanket and pillow and went down the hall to the kitchen. She knew there were still things stored in the pantry and root cellar that she could eat, even without making a fire. A ham hung from the ceiling in the cool cellar and she cut off a piece to go with the crackers she found in the pantry. An apple from the basket and a slice of cheese from the brick on the shelf would serve very nicely for breakfast. Later she would go to a café for a hot cup of tea. She cleaned the table after her breakfast, carefully disposing of any telltale crumbs. She had no idea when the bank's inspectors might decide to go through the house and took care to leave everything exactly as it was.

Not for the first time, Marianne wished she had been born a male. An heir to the title and the property would have made all the difference. Instead, the title – if her father was not alive or could not be found – would pass to a distant cousin she had never met. The heir had been notified of the earl's disappearance and was quite likely traveling from wherever he was to assume the property. Before that happened, Marianne intended to know where her father was and why he disappeared. Nothing formal could happen until he had been gone for a determined period of time—she wasn't sure what that period was – and then the Will could be read and property disposed of.

All she could be sure of having was the small trust she inherited from her mother, and that was not available to her for another two months on her 21st birthday. In the meantime, when the distant cousin showed up, and learned that Marianne was not among the missing with her father, she would be totally dependent upon his "good graces" and sense of responsibility to take care of his predecessor's daughter. She shuddered as she realized that she could be handily married off to the first male her cousin came across, and she would have no say in the matter at all. As her guardian, it was his right. This had happened several times to friends she knew. Usually it was the parents who arranged marriages, and often they took their daughter's feelings into consideration, but occasionally a young woman would be simply married off, with no say in the matter, to a man of the father or guardian's choosing. None of these, as far as she knew, had happy marriages. Her only real chance was to find her father.

Thomas Austin Beckworth, Earl of Worthingham, was known as a responsible, sensible man. He had a seat in Parliament, was well liked and respected, and no one suspected any foul play in his disappearance. In fact, he packed his bags, took his best pair of matched grays and open carriage, and left on what he told Marianne, in his last note to her, was a short one week journey to see a friend in the next county. He never arrived at the friend's house, and literally disappeared into thin air, his carriage and grays with him.

It was easier to slip into the deserted house than to slip out in the daylight. Marianne left by the back door from the kitchen, went through the garden and the copse of woods behind the house, and emerged onto the street in back. It was unlikely that anyone would see her there since there was only one house nearby and it had been closed for the winter, the owners having removed to the country until spring.

Before spending the day in the library, Marianne walked to the nearby cottage where her old nurse, Nana, lived. Nana was the only person Marianne trusted these days. There Marianne had left her meager supply of clothing brought with her from the country, and Nana knew where she spent her nights. She wanted a wash and a change of clothing before venturing out into the world. Despite the trust she had in her old nurse, she was reluctant to share the information about the letters, at least until she had read them herself.

Clean and in fresh dress, Marianne settled herself in the public library at her usual corner table in the very back of the building. The sunlight streaming in the tall windows made it easy to read the dull faded script. She started with the oldest letter, dated May 1881, less than seven months ago. This was the letter that started *"My dearest Tom."*

"I know we agreed not to correspond, but you should know that your brother is extremely unwell. The doctor has recently been and seems to feel that John cannot continue to survive much longer. I urge you to consider visiting before it is too late. Since the passing of your beloved wife, we thought we would hear from you regarding what you planned to do about the situation. Decisions need to be made quickly, and I await your correspondence or visit. As always, Angelique."

Marianne was puzzled. She had no idea her father had a brother. She had been told that her grandparents had died many years before, but no mention was ever made about any siblings.

The letter was franked in Cambridge, which was not that distant. Despite the salutation, it was far from the love letter that she had expected. She took a deep breath, and opened the second letter, dated two months later.

"Tom, your cheque arrived and was much appreciated. However, what we need from you now is your support and information about your plans. John hovers on the verge of another outburst, and I do the best I can to keep him calm and comfortable. However, you know how he is when he is agitated, and lately he has been impossible to keep quiet. He speaks of the child frequently in his ravings. Please come. You need to speak to each other before the end."

The third letter, dated in September, was even more pleading:

"Please, Tom, it is urgent that you come at once. Your brother needs to see you and hear from your lips what is happening. He seems to have more lucid days lately, although the doctor is not very encouraging. An old woman in the neighborhood gave me some herbs. They seem to be helping,

but she has assured me that they cannot cure him, only prolong his life… and perhaps his suffering. Still, he insists that he see you and speak to you before he goes to his final rest."

The final letter was dated a mere two weeks before her father disappeared.

"Thank you for your assurance that you will arrive soon. We know you have duties there and much to see to before making the journey, which will change all of our lives considerably. This is for the best, Tom. Perhaps if we all put our heads together, we can turn this bad situation around. I know the world cannot know about John, but surely the child must be told the truth. Knowing you are coming has calmed your brother and he is patiently awaiting your arrival. He says he will be able to let go once he speaks with you, as there are things you must be told that even I do not know."

Again, it was signed *"as always, Angelique"*. The child…was she, Marianne, the child the letters speak of? A cold feeling of dread came over her and she shuddered. Nevertheless, she knew she would have to travel to Cambridge to seek out this elusive and hitherto unknown brother and there, hopefully, find not only her father, but the truth.

The funds brought with her from the country estate were nearly depleted, and Marianne would have to make one more trip to the house. In the meantime, she desperately needed a cup of tea and there were several hours before she could slip into the house undetected. Her clothing, being dark and plain, hid her identity well, particularly when she covered her hair with a scarf, so the lack of a companion was not noted with any interest. She arranged for a ticket on the mail coach for the journey, which she estimated would take two days. Traveling by public conveyance would cause less notice, as she could be a governess or teacher going to her next assignment. She spent another hour over tea, purchased a few necessities and a small gift of gratitude for Nana, and then returned to her nurse's cottage to pack.

"Nana," Marianne began as they sat at the table over tea and scones. "Did you know my father had a brother?"

Nana looked up, startled. "Whatever gave you that idea, child?" she asked.

"I know he does, but I wanted to know if you knew about John." Marianne said casually, reaching for another scone.

Nana was obviously flustered. She busied herself buttering the scone and sipping her tea. Marianne shrewdly observed her behavior and was certain that Nana had information she needed to know.

"Nana," she said quietly, "Father left to go to his brother, who is very ill. I don't know exactly where he is, but I intend to find both of them. You need to tell me what you know."

"I can't, Mari, I promised." Nana looked at her guiltily.

"Yes, you can," Marianne responded, "and you must. This will help me find my father and put everything to right. I cannot let a distant cousin take over my father's property and title without a fight. I need to find him quickly. I leave tomorrow morning on the mail coach for Cambridge, but I think you know where I have to go from there to find them."

Tears welled up in the old woman's eyes. "Let it be, child," she said. "Nothing good can come of this."

"If you won't help me, then I will just have to find them myself. "

"I can see you are determined and nothing will sway you. I'll tell you what I can. The name you are looking for is John Forrest. He is outside Cambridge several miles to the east. Your father won't thank you for interfering. He needs to take care of the situation in his own way."

"What situation?" Marianne asked, but Nana clamped her lips shut and refused to say any more.

Marianne slipped through the copse of woods and then through the back kitchen door. She didn't stop to light a candle but found her way through the hallway into the library. Once there, she quickly shut the drapes and lit the lamp, then moved to the painting on the wall behind the desk to expose a small safe. Even though it had been years, Marianne remembered the combination and found a substantial stash of coins inside. There was more than enough for her purposes, but she took them all, wanting to be prepared for any emergency.

The mail coach left at 6 AM, so she hurriedly made up her bed on the sofa and attempted to get some sleep. Her mind wouldn't shut down enough and she tossed and turned for hours, finally dozing off, only to come awake in a panic, sure she had missed the coach. The clock on the wall assured her it was only 5 am, and she rose, tidied up the room, dressed and repacked her bag. A quick trip to the kitchen and pantry to break her fast, and she was ready to slip out the back door again.

The valise was quite light but seemed to become heavier the farther she walked. She arrived at the inn just as the coach was loading, handed them her bag and was able to get a quick cup of hot tea before the passengers were called aboard. Once the mail coach left the city, Marianne breathed a sigh of relief, tucked her reticule behind her on the seat, and dozed off for the first hour of the trip to catch up on some much-needed sleep.

The coach only held two passengers…Marianne and an older woman, Emily, who told Marianne she was going to visit her daughter in Cambridge. It was a long journey, but the woman was friendly and they discussed herbs and cooking; Emily had no hint that Marianne was anything but the governess she claimed.

When the coach stopped at the Red Bore Inn for the night and the driver bespoke rooms for his passengers, Marianne was more than ready to alight and walk around. After a plain but filling supper, she retired for the night, rather amused that she was finally sleeping in a bed.

The next morning, there were several more passengers besides her and Emily, and the coach was quite crowded. Marianne was wedged between the door and a middle aged, bearded man who had obviously spent the night drinking, if the odor from his breath and body were any indication. There was a farm woman who coughed every few minutes and a very thin man who kept his head down most of the time. Fortunately, the remainder of the trip was only a few hours, and by the time they reached their destination, Marianne was quite nauseated from the odors she had been subjected to during their four-hour journey. She was very thankful to descend into clean air once again. Emily apparently was met by her daughter, a robust young woman with a child in tow, and the lady wished her traveling-companion the best in her new position before leaving.

The coach driver directed her to a bed and breakfast just down the street, where Marianne was able to obtain a room for a very reasonable amount. She was relieved that she did not have to bundle herself with scarves to avoid being identified as the earl's daughter. Surely there were few people here who had ever heard of her, and none would expect her to be in Cambridge.

The landlady was no help when Marianne inquired about a John Forrest but suggested that the telegraph office might know of him. Inquiries there, and at the post office and again at the local mercantile store all turned up no information.

Marianne spent two days asking everyone she met, but no one had ever heard of the man. She inquired at the local livery to see if perhaps her father had left his coach or grays there when he first arrived in Cambridge. Again, there was no information and no one had seen the earl. Each night she had the same disturbing dream...her father confined to a bed and asking her for help.

She was sitting in the local restaurant at dinner one evening when she heard a conversation behind her. A young woman was speaking with the man who was seated at the table. When he called her "Angelique," Marianne suddenly came to full attention, turned and looked at the woman. Angelique was not a very common name, and she thought it unusual enough to stop the women as she left the restaurant. The woman was very attractive with deep red hair and green eyes.

"Excuse me," Marianne said, "But I wonder if you could help me. I'm looking for John Forrest or the Earl of Worthingham. Do you by any chance know either of them?"

Startled, the young woman stared at Marianne, then shook her head and walked swiftly out the door. Marianne, finding this behavior strange, went to the door after her but she had disappeared. She then tuned to the gentleman seated at the table who had spoken Angelique's name.

"I have something for Angelique, the woman you were just speaking with, " Marianne invented. "But I was not able to catch her. Apparently she was in a very big hurry. There is a family heirloom I am commissioned to deliver into her hands."

"I can give you her direction," said the man, helpfully. And he carefully wrote out the address and directions on a piece of paper.

"Thank you so much. I am in your debt." Marianne took the paper and left quickly. She scanned the information, noting that it was several miles out of town. That did make sense to her, coinciding with the little amount of information from Nana, and she felt that she had finally found what she was looking for, but didn't understand why the woman denied knowing John or her father.

Ordinarily, she would not have left town that late in the day, but her intuition told her she needed to go immediately if she wanted to find her father. Without hesitation, she hired a carriage and horse and left town for the address on the paper.

It was close to sunset when she arrived at large house set far back from the road. When she knocked on the door, she was not surprised to see the woman from the restaurant open the door. Apparently the woman was not surprised to see Marianne, either, as she opened the door and invited her inside.

"You're Marianne, I assume," began Angelique. At her guest's nod, she continued, "I think we better have a chat before I take you upstairs,"

"I don't know how you found out about John or where your father is, but I want to assure you that Tom will be fine," Angelique continued, taking Marianne's cloak and bag. She led her into the sitting room and indicated a chair beside the blazing fireplace. 'It was a serious accident, but he is recovering nicely."

"Accident?" exclaimed Marianne.

"Did you think he would desert you for no good reason? I contacted Tom for his brother's sake, and he was in a carriage accident on the way here. He was unconscious for several days and has been fretting about you and hoping you were still safely in the country."

"My father disappeared, and the whole countryside assumes he is not coming back. The authorities have notified his heir, a distant cousin. No one knows I am here, or indeed that I was not with him on this trip. Please take me to see my father." Marianne did not reveal that her dreams had led her to discover he was missing.

"In a moment. First I need to apologize for my actions in the restaurant. I was taken by surprise and didn't know what to say to you.

Tom said you wouldn't take my denial and would probably find a way to come out here. He has great faith in your capabilities, my dear."

"What is the situation with his brother? I didn't even know I had an uncle. Why is that?"

"Tom will explain it all in good time."

"I understand he is ill. What exactly is wrong with him?"

"John suffers from a strange malady," Angelique said softly. "Sometimes he is upset over nothing at all. Sometimes he is sad and just sits and cries. Sometimes he seems perfectly normal, but one never knows when he will be any of those things. He has been almost himself while Tom has been here, and spent many nights sitting by the bed talking to him."

Marianne suddenly had a strange feeling in the pit of her stomach. Hesitantly she asked, "How old is John?"

The answer confirmed her worst fears. John was the older brother. John was really the earl. All this time her father had been living a lie. Was John part of the lie, or did he not know his brother had taken his title and land?

"Of course John knows. It was his idea." Angelique answered the question before Marianne could ask it.

"But why?"

"John knew he could not manage the lands and the responsibilities that come with the title because of his illness. He arranged to be reported as killed in the war so Tom could assume the earldom. John wanted to just disappear from society…he couldn't live having people point to him as a freak. No one suspects that he is even alive and we had planned to make sure that no one found out by never communicating with Tom. However, when the situation became critical, we both felt Tom needed to know."

"I found your letters," Marianne admitted quietly. "Now I only have one question. Am I the child mentioned?"

"Yes, you are. Tom will have to tell you the rest. Come, we'll go up to see them both now."

Angelique carried the lamp and they ascended the stairs. It was an old house, but quite elegant. Marianne was led into a large comfortable room and immediately saw her father lying on the bed under a quilt, exactly as she had seen him in her dreams.

It was a tearful reunion and she barely noticed the man sitting on the other side of the bed. When she looked up, she found him staring at her. He seemed very familiar to her, but she thought it was because he resembled his brother.

"This is John," Angelique said, and John stood and extended his hand. He did look very ill, and much older than her father.

"Marianne," said the earl. "There are things you need to know that I could not tell you before, but it is time now. Please come sit by my bed."

"I'll have dinner prepared for all of us. Tom, are you up to coming downstairs or should I have a tray sent up?" Angelique stood and prepared to leave the room.

"A tray, I think, and perhaps Marianne will join me, and John also. We have much to discuss."

The next few hours were a painful revelation to Marianne. As she had surmised, and Angelique had confirmed, John should actually have been the earl. He chose to fake his death on the battlefield, which was not really very difficult, in order that his brother could assume the title at the passing of their father. Even their parents had not been aware that John was still very much alive.

The biggest shock to Marianne, however, was when Tom gently revealed that she was, in fact, John's child. He assured her that he and his wife had loved her dearly as if she were their own, and that the trust fund set up by his wife was, in fact, hers on her 21st birthday. John had married while overseas, but to a woman that English society would never accept as wife of an earl. She died in childbirth and John brought the baby home to his brother and sister-in-law, who despaired of having children of their own.

"My red hair?" Marianne inquired.

"Like your birth mother." John replied quietly. "I wanted you to be brought up with all the advantages of your birthright. Tom and Mary wanted children desperately and they have loved you as their own since you were a tiny babe. Make no mistake; they are your real parents."

"And who is Angelique?"

"My Katy's younger sister. She has been devoted to me since I returned to England and has cared for me through the many crises with my health." He coughed painfully. "I fear she will not have to care for me much longer."

It was late when Angelique came for Marianne to take her to her room, who was more than ready for bed. The trip, emotions, and the turmoil in her mind with all the information she had been given had taken its toll and she was nearly falling asleep in the chair.

"Your father will be much stronger tomorrow, Mari. Your room is ready and I think you need a long night's sleep. I won't wake you tomorrow…just sleep as long as you can. We don't want you falling ill also."

Angelique led her to a pleasant room down the hall. She was too tired to even notice the elegant furnishings, the beautiful quilt on the bed or the flowers on the nightstand. Marianne removed her shoes and dress, fell into bed wearing only her shift, and was fast asleep almost before her head hit the pillow.

Dreams had always seemed to give her information she needed, and they did not fail her this time. She dreamed of her birth mother, saw her as a carefree, beautiful Gypsy woman with flowing red hair who blew her kisses. She saw John as he was twenty odd years ago, suffering with his strange malady, but deeply in love with his wife. She saw how happy Tom and Mary were and how welcoming they were to the baby and had no doubt as to their unconditional love.

Then her dream changed, and she saw herself as a much older woman with several children around her…her grandchildren. Even in the dream, she questioned how she could ever have grandchildren when she was not married and had no prospects. Again it changed, and she saw the earl walking her down the aisle toward the man she was marrying, although all she could see of the man's face was his beautiful green eyes. Strangely, she saw in her dream John and Angelique dancing at her wedding. She smiled in her sleep, turned over and fell into a dreamless state until almost ten the next morning.

Angelique was right…Tom was much better the next morning and felt that he probably could travel by the next day. The doctor called and agreed that another day's rest would not hurt, but that he was basically back to normal. The previous doctor had retired, and this one had not examined John previously. His diagnosis was that John was suffering from a lung malady which might or might not prove fatal.

From her years in the country, Marianne had become quite proficient in using herbs, both in cooking and for healing purposes. An old woman on the estate taught her a great deal and Marianne insisted on gathering herbs from the garden and woods for a poultice for John's chest. She brewed a tea which he drank under protest, but which seemed to stop the cough and ease his symptoms.

"You're not dying," Marianne assured him. "I saw you dancing at my wedding."

John looked startled. "When are you getting married? Tom never said a word."

Marianne laughed. "I don't know…haven't found the groom yet, but I dreamed you were at my wedding."

John smiled. "My Katy also had dreams," he said, "and perhaps you are fey, like she was."

"My dreams brought me here, "Marianne admitted. "I dreamed Father was calling for me and was hurt. I dreamed he showed me the desk where I found Angelique's letters. If I dream about what herbs you should take," she teased, "will you take them?"

John smiled. "Of course. I will trust anything my niece gives me to take." With those words, he released her as his daughter and became her uncle in fact, and Marianne was both moved and grateful. For the life of her, she couldn't relate to anyone other than Tom as her father… or Mary as her mother, for that matter.

Before they left the next morning, Marianne made a list of the herbs and instructions for preparing them for Angelique to use for John. Then after a fond and somewhat tearful farewell, Tom and Marianne left for London. The carriage had been repaired after the accident; the grays had not been injured and were ready and eager for the trip.

It was an uneventful two-day journey and they arrived in London, prepared to oust the distant cousin from the title and property. Fortunately, he had not yet arrived, but Tom was vocal in his criticism of the bank for having the house cleared of furniture and his potential heir notified just because he was "a few days late" in returning. (No one dared point out that the "few days" were more like three months or that he had never arrived at his stated destination.) With much scrambling, the house was returned to its former state by the next day. The bankers were able to track down most of the house staff and bring them back to work. The official explanation for his weeks of being among the missing was that he had been injured in an accident and was taken in by a farm couple in a remote area, who had no means of communication.

The distant cousin arrived the following week. He called upon the bankers, only to be told that the earl had returned and they apologized profusely for his inconvenience. Brian Stokely was not in the least perturbed by not becoming an earl. In fact, he had found the prospect rather disheartening. He did not need the funds, as he was quite well off in his own right. He was never really "into" titles, had been dragging his feet, as it were, in coming to London, and was very well pleased that the earl had turned up, hale and hearty.

Brian called upon the earl to pay his respects before traveling back to Birmingham. The butler showed him into the drawing room and went off to announce him to the earl. In the meantime, Marianne, not aware of the company, entered the drawing room in search of a book she had been reading and was surprised to find a tall, blonde, good-looking gentleman, hat in hand, standing by the fireplace.

"Oh, excuse me," she exclaimed. "I assume Thompson has gone to find my father?"

"I believe he has," Brian replied rather solemnly. He couldn't help but stare at the beautiful sight before him. He had never been attracted to red hair before, but he found Marianne absolutely charming.

Quickly she ducked her head and backed out of the room, forgetting the book she was looking for. She almost backed into the earl, who was on his way in to greet Brian.

"Marianne, come meet Brian Stokely, my heir," said Tom, extending his hand to his guest.

"I want you to know, sir, that I am very happy that you have returned in good health. I was not looking forward to assuming this responsibility for a good many years yet." Brian pumped his hand enthusiastically.

"Ah, well, one never knows what life will bring," said the earl, with a chuckle. "We would be most pleased if you would join us for dinner this evening."

With his eyes on Marianne, Brian readily accepted the invitation. Marianne blushed, curtsied and excused herself to notify Cook that they had a guest. On her way to the kitchen, she scolded herself for becoming so flustered. She was not unused to having guests, although it had been three years since she played hostess to her father. It would be an interesting dinner, she suspected. She liked Brian Stokely right away but wondered why he seemed so familiar to her.

Perhaps it had something to do with his eyes, which were exactly like the eyes in her dream – the beautiful green eyes of the man that waited for her on her wedding day.

The Waiting

She leaned wearily against the pillar at the corner of the porch, a tall gaunt woman in a thin patched dress, looking considerably older than her thirty-five years. The once strong boards beneath her feet were now rotting and the porch pillar flaked with faded paint.

She gazed out across the fields as her mind moved back to the time when her husband lovingly worked the earth in those fields. For a moment, she allowed herself to dwell on that happier time and could almost see Ben's broad strong back bending and moving as he tilled the soil. Many times in the past she had stood in this same spot, leaning against the pillar, dreaming happily of the future.

Kate brought herself back to the present with difficulty and became aware of her body's need for food. You can't bring back the past or rush the future, she thought. Ben had often said, "Katie girl, today is today… live it like there's no tomorrow." With a sigh, she wiped her work-worn hands on the sides of her dress and walked briskly to the door, already focusing on the dark bread in the kitchen bread box and planning to rise early to bake another supply in the coolness of the morning.

Kate opened her eyes slowly, reluctant to disturb her warm cocoon under the heavy patch-work quilt. She lay without moving, listening to the predawn chirping of the birds as they welcomed the new day. A faint breeze disturbed the curtains that were once bright with red flowers but which she could see, even in the dim half-darkness, were sun-faded to a blotchy pink. She closed her eyes again briefly for her morning prayer to thank God for the new day and her blessings, although she would have been hard-pressed to name them had she been asked to do so. Her prayer finished, she flung back the covers and swung her feet to the floor, reaching in the same motion for her dress which lay across the foot of the bed.

Before the sky was pink with the coming dawn, Kate had splashed water on her face and had run the comb through her pale, brown hair, twisting it into a neat bun at the back of her head. The heat of the oven took the chill off the crisp autumn air in the kitchen. She punched down the dough that had swollen to a pregnant mound overnight, patted it into a loaf and covered the pan with a damp cloth for the final rising. She hummed as she filled the kettle from the hand pump at the kitchen sink and set it on the stove for tea.

As the sun edged its way above the horizon, Kate sat at the kitchen table, hands wrapped around the brown earthenware cup, sipping her tea. The kitchen smelled of baking bread and she breathed deeply, loving the odor, the sun, the tree outside the window with its red and gold leaves making cheerful patches among the green. The cow had been milked and the foamy, white liquid was cooling in the cellar. Since she first opened her eyes this morning, she had nursed a feeling of excited expectancy. Kate had never discounted her intuition. She had lived with a feeling of impending tragedy for two days before Ben had been struck down by a falling tree in a storm. Today she instinctively felt it was an occasion for celebrating and she would simply make sure all her chores were done. Then she would wait for whatever was going to happen.

As she chopped the vegetables for a savory stew, Kate debated for a moment about adding the last of the dried venison. There was really no question in her mind, even though she faced the long winter without meat. The Lord would provide, as He always had. After Ben died two years ago, the neighbors brought her beef and some vegetables, which she canned and stored in neat rows in the cellar. Last year a deer was caught in the pasture fence. Without a qualm, she shot it and dragged it home. With the help of a neighbor boy, they hung it in the barn away from wolves and other scavengers. Then she skinned it, salted and preserved the meat and was well fed all winter and summer. Something would surely take care of her food problems again so she wasn't worried.

Her day was filled with the many chores of the tiny farm. There was the garden to be weeded, the last of the ripened tomatoes to pick, and the cow to be milked again. The barn, although only a badly constructed shed, needed patching and cleaning. Yet the persistent feeling remained like an unspoken promise and permeated her entire existence. Had the sun always felt this warm and pleasant? Had the sky always been such a beautiful blue? This day her senses were keenly aware of every sound, every color.... every second that passed.

It was nearly sunset when Kate seated herself in the rocker and gazed out across the prairie, unconsciously rubbing her aching left arm as she gently rocked back and forth. Far to the west she could see a tiny cloud of dust that was growing slowly. She watched it with a suppressed feeling of excitement but with no sign of alarm or surprise. After a time, she went into the house to stir the stew and put the loaf of fresh bread on the ledge above the stove to warm. Carefully she spooned the remains of the precious ground coffee into the pot. It had been a long time since she had tasted coffee, but visitors were a rare and special occasion, and the cloud of dust was undoubtedly heading her way.

By the time the dust materialized into a lone rider on horseback, it was almost dusk. The stranger dismounted in front of the porch with a cheerful greeting. As he pushed his hat back on his head and looked up at Kate, his hands on dungareed hips. Her face registered amazement and surprise. By appearance the man standing before her could have been her late husband's brother - right down to his steel blue eyes that crinkled when he smiled! Kate's eyes suddenly filled with tears and the unaccustomed emotion seemed to render her speechless.

After he had respectfully inquired about the possibility of hospitality, she waved her hand helplessly toward the barn and then pointed to the door behind her from which the delicious aroma of warm bread, savory stew and freshly made coffee drifted. The stranger smiled again, touched his hat in gesture of respect and led his mount toward the barn.

He was back before Kate had time to set the table and dish up the stew, but the interval was long enough to give her time to collect her emotions and scold herself for allowing her imagination to take over. Of course her memories were faded…of course he only slightly resembled her Ben…it must just have been a trick of the twilight.

Her guest soon put her at ease over the meal, speaking in a soft drawl and telling her stories of his adventures on the trail. Kate found herself telling him about Ben and how she had managed without him. She spoke of her good neighbors and about the deer caught in the fence. Having been without a good listener for so long, she didn't realize her face had become pretty with animation. Her occasional laugh of delight at his tales was musical and youthful. Serious incidents in her life became humorous with the telling and her natural wit, long unused, proved as keen as ever.

It was an odd feeling to share her thoughts and feelings with a stranger. Stranger? Somehow Kate couldn't associate that word with her companion. Often a gesture or expression of the man across her table would suddenly remind her of her husband, and she would catch her breath with a slight pang.

They sat over coffee for hours---laughing, talking about everything and anything, just as she and Ben used to do. Kate had not been so happy and relaxed for many, many months. She did not want to think about tomorrow or the future. Perhaps this was what she had been waiting for all day---this pleasant interlude in her lonely existence. Yet something told her it was not quite all it seemed.

At one point, she started to rise to clear the dishes from the table, but he stopped her with a light touch on her arm, a smile, and a gentle shake of his head. The dishes stayed on the table as he moved across the room to the fireplace. She followed, relaxed in a chair and watched admiringly as her guest expertly lay the logs and lighted the fire before sitting down in Ben's chair.

It was late when they finally stopped talking and he stood up. The firelight flickered across his face, catching the bronze highlights in his hair. As Kate raised her eyes to his, she felt mesmerized and suddenly realized why she had that feeling of anticipation, why he reminded her so strongly of Ben and even what he was going to say to her.

"It's time, Katie girl. Are you ready?" She swallowed hard, smiled and nodded. Then she took the strong brown hand that Ben extended to her, knowing that her intuition had been right once again.

The neighbor boy stopped by Kate's house the next morning to deliver some extra vegetables from his mother's garden. He heard the cow in the barn, lowing in pain. Having been born and bred on the farm, he grabbed the milk pail from the porch and ran to the barn, relieving the animal of her painfully swollen udder. Then he headed to the house, expecting to find its owner still sleeping, or perhaps ill and unable to get out of bed.

He found Kate, still sitting by the cold fireplace, and noticed with curiosity that the table was set for two, although only one plate bore the remains of food. They said she must have had a heart attack, but couldn't have had any pain, as there was such a peaceful and contented look on her face---almost a smile. But then, they said, perhaps it was a blessing for her, poor thing, not to have to face another hard cold winter alone now that her man had been gone these past two years.

Out of respect for Kate, no one mentioned the extra, unused plate at the table except the curious neighbor boy who was quickly hushed by his elders. After all, women living alone on the prairie sometimes have strange delusions, they say.

Grandpa's Gift

"Honey, you really should eat something," called her mother from the bottom of the stairs. Moriah didn't respond. She just curled up on her bed hugging her teddy bear while the tears ran down her face. She had been in her room almost three days, ever since her mother gently broke the news.

It just wasn't fair. Her grandfather couldn't be dead. She had been looking forward to spending the summer with him in just two weeks, as soon as school was over.

Grandpa was the only one who really listened to Moriah. He seemed to know everything. If she wanted to know about America, Grandpa knew, and he wove such marvelous tales about the Wild West she could almost believe she had seen it herself. If she wanted to know about crossing the Channel from England, his description was so vivid she could almost feel she was on a boat with the salt spray in her face. She used to believe he could do magic, but her mother explained that her grandfather was very good at "sleight of hand," and the things he did were really just tricks. She believed her mother, but she liked to pretend Grandpa was magic anyway. Now he was gone, and Moriah couldn't believe she would never see him again!

Just two weeks ago, Grandpa had sent his carriage to bring her to his house just outside London for an unscheduled visit. That was a pleasant surprise, but it was a rather strange outing. It was almost as if he knew he wouldn't see her again. They had a wonderful day, playing cards and sharing a pot of their favorite tea. Grandpa told her more stories…about his childhood and his parents and her grandmother, who had passed away before she was born.

"Do you miss Grandma a lot?" asked Moriah, noticing the far-away look in her grandfather's eyes when he talked about his late wife.

"Of course I do, child. But she is still with me in my heart, and I will see her again someday… soon." At the time, Moriah didn't understand what her grandfather was talking about. Oh, she knew what they taught in church and all…about seeing our loved ones again when we die, but her father had passed away when she was little and she barely remembered what he looked like. She couldn't honestly say she really missed him and rarely even thought about him. She had never lost anyone really close to her, so she had no point of reference.

Just before he sent her home, her grandfather gave her something he had always treasured… a beautiful stein, trimmed in silver with a shiny silver top and a lovely picture of a cabin by a river painted on the side. Moriah had always admired the stein which he kept in the china closet in the dining room. But as many stories as he told her, the only thing Grandpa had ever said about it was that it was gift from his father.

"The stein is now yours, my child," said the old man. "May you find as much comfort in it as I have." Moriah promised she would always treasure it but didn't really understand how it could be a "comfort" to her. When she questioned Grandpa, he just smiled and hugged her tightly before sending her home, her new gift wrapped safely in a cloth.

Her mother came upstairs to try to persuade her to come downstairs and eat, but left again, shaking her head. She decided to let the child grieve a while longer, since Moriah had been so very close to her grandfather. It was difficult to lose one you love, but especially at such a young age. Fourteen was not easy, being on the verge between childhood and womanhood. But time was a great healer, as she had found after losing her husband and her own father several years before. Her daughter would be fine…she just needed some time.

Darkness fell, and still Moriah lay curled up on her bed. She was too depressed to light the lamp. She had no desire or energy to even get undressed and put on her pajamas. Silent tears turned into sobs, and after a time, she cried herself to sleep.

When she awoke, the moonlight was streaming in the window. She didn't know what time it was or what had caused her to awaken. For a moment, she didn't remember about Grandpa and then it came back to her in a rush.

As her eyes filled with tears, she saw the moonlight from the full moon illuminating the chest of drawers, and her grandfather's stein sitting on top seemed to glow. Moriah wiped her tears away, sat up in bed and stared at the stein. Yes, it was definitely glowing. Perhaps it was just the way the moonlight fell on the silver top. No, it seemed that the entire stein was glowing! She slipped out of bed and walked to the chest of drawers, a bit puzzled about what was causing the shimmering light.

As she lifted it down from the top of the chest, she was amazed to see that there was something different about the picture on the front. Looking closely, she realized that the smoke from the chimney of the cabin and the campfire on the riverbank both appeared to be moving. The river was flowing, and the dogs by the canoe were wagging their tales. The whole scene had come to life! Excited and fascinated, she touched the picture gingerly.

Suddenly, Moriah was standing on the riverbank by the campfire in front of the cabin. The two dogs ran up to her, tongues lolling and tales wagging. In a daze, she knelt to pet them, when the cabin door opened and her beloved Grandpa came out.

"So, you found the secret of the magic stein, child," he commented, as she flung herself in his arms. Tears and grief were forgotten as she breathed in the familiar scent of pipe tobacco on his shirt and felt his beard ruffle her hair.

"Grandpa, how can this be," she cried, clinging to his familiar figure

"Come inside and I'll explain, my child," said the old man. Eagerly she followed him inside, holding tightly to his hand. He bade her sit by the table and he sat down in the chair in front of her.

"Many years ago," he began, "My father told me this cabin was his favorite place in the world, so he had it painted on a stein. He told me he used to visit the cabin whenever he wanted, just by touching the picture when the full moon made it shimmer. When he passed on, he left it to me and I discovered I could visit him at the cabin the same way.

"Eventually the pain of his passing faded, and so did the need to visit him at the cabin. Now you have the stein, and someday you will pass it along to someone you love."

"Oh, Grandpa," cried Moriah. "I will always want to come and see you here. I won't ever stop coming to see you."

"Moriah, my child, there will come a time when I will be a loving memory in your heart. That is part of life. We do have to let go of our loved ones who must leave us, you know, but it's not forever. You must have faith, little one, that someday we will all be together again." The old man squeezed Moriah's hand tightly. "But for now, we can enjoy our visits. You will be able to come to the cabin whenever there is a full moon. Part of the pain of missing our loved ones is worrying that they are not well or happy. Just remember, when you and I are not together, I am with your grandmother."

Grandpa showed Moriah the inside of the cabin, the sleeping loft at the top of the ladder, and the wooden carvings he was working on. They went outside and Moriah played with the dogs for a while. He told her that the dogs were his companions when he was a young boy. Then they all waded in the shallows of the river. All the while, he told her more wonderful stories, just as he always did. Grandpa made their favorite tea, and a plate of raspberry scones, telling her that he knew she had not been eating and that would have to stop. She laughed and devoured the scones, her appetite having suddenly returned.

Too soon it was time for Moriah to leave. She could see the sun setting on the other side of the trees, and somehow she knew it was time to go home. Grandpa showed her a painting on the wall over the fireplace that she had not noticed before. It was a picture of Moriah's bedroom. She was surprised to see her bed and teddy bear, and her chest of drawers with the stein sitting on top.

Grandpa hugged her and then said, "Remember I will always love you, my child. Now put your hand on the painting, Moriah." She did so and immediately found herself back in her own bed. The sky was just beginning to show signs of dawn.

Was it all just a dream? No, it definitely wasn't, she thought, grinning as she brushed the crumbs of the raspberry scones from her shirt. She snuggled down in her bed, smiled to herself, said, "I love you, too, Grandpa..."

But the magic of the stein would have to be a secret, just between her and her grandfather. She knew her mother would never believe it, and might even take the stein away, and Moriah couldn't let that happen. Yawning sleepily, she decided to start a journal so she could remember all the things she wanted to share with Grandpa on her next visit.

Still smiling, Moriah closed her eyes and went to sleep.

The Little Green Pony

"She's doing it again," said Alice in a low voice. She was sitting on one end of the sofa with a book in her lap, attempting to read. Her husband sat at the other end, eyes glued to the TV, flipping the remote from one station to another.

"Doing what?" Joe didn't take his eyes off the TV and continued scanning.

"You know what. When I picked her up from school today, she said she liked Mrs. Abbott better than her old first grade teacher."

"So?' The remote continued to click. His eyes never left the screen.

Alice gave up the pretense of reading. She put her book on the coffee table.

"Mrs. Abbott is the only first grade teacher she ever had. I met her the first day of school. There is no other first grade teacher there."

"Oh." Joe sighed and put down the remote. "I thought we were all over that. Honey, I don't know what to tell you. The kid has a really great imagination."

"It's more than imagination, Joe, and you know it!" Alice was becoming agitated and Joe slid over and put his arm around her shoulders.

"We'll deal with it, honey. Maybe we can find a doctor…"

"The last one told me I was the one with the problem. He blamed it on normal childhood imagination, too, but it's not…you know it's not!"

"OK, OK. She hasn't done it for a while. Maybe this will all go away. Just ignore it for now."

Emma was six years old, a sweet and loving child. She was very intelligent for her age, knew her colors and numbers by the time she was two, never had tantrums or was disobedient. She was a perfect child…almost. The only problem her parents had was what her father tried to call her vivid imagination. Except the things the child said and did were chillingly related to another child…a child that had died in a fire almost seven years before.

Alice and Joe's first daughter, Sally, had been eight years old when a fire raged through their house. Alice had been pregnant at the time, and Joe got her out of the house and went back for Sally, who had been following them out. He never reached her. He was burned severely and spent several weeks in the hospital. Everything was lost, including all of their belongings, pictures, clothing…they were literally left with nothing but the clothes on their back. But their greatest loss was their beloved daughter.

Through the goodness of neighbors, friends and the local media, Alice and Joe put their lives back together. Benefits were held to collect funds to help the destitute couple. Family members donated pictures and memorabilia since they had lost all record of their previous life. Alice carefully put them in an album and then put it away, finding it too painful to have around.

Alice and Joe both suffered from bouts of depression, missed their daughter terribly, but finally were able to focus on the coming birth. It was a girl, with golden curls and blue eyes very similar to Sally's. They finally came to terms with the loss of their first-born and turned their eyes to the future.

Emma was walking and talking rather early for her age. She had quite an extensive vocabulary by the time she was two. Both her parents were very proud of the fact that she learned things so quickly, and Sesame Street received the credit for her ability to name colors and count at such an early age. Emma didn't like to sleep in the dark…there was always a night light in the hall for her…and the one thing that terrified her was fire. This was not unusual, they were told. Actually, Alice herself was understandably paranoid about fire, and the doctor explained that Emma simply picked up on her mother's fear.

The first disturbing incident occurred at Emma's third birthday party. After the presents were opened and the three children left, Emma asked where Max was. "Who's Max?" asked her father.

"Last time I was three you got me a big dog," explained Emma. "I want another big dog this time just like Max."

Alice's face lost all color. Joe, never having been privy to the names of his daughter's toys (either daughter), looked puzzled but promised to see if he could find a big stuffed dog for her.

That was only the first of many comments Emma made that disturbed and upset Alice. Joe was usually not around when these incidents happened, and he tended to brush off Alice's feelings about them. "Coincidence" or "great imagination" was his two most common explanations. He even bluntly said he thought his wife was reading more into normal childhood imagination than there was. Alice, having been through childhood fantasies with one daughter, knew the difference. Emma continued to offer strange comments on occasion, usually when her mother least expected it.

Alice was cleaning out a storage closet one Saturday afternoon. Five-year-old Emma was playing with her toys in the corner. Then, bored, she started poking around some of the boxes.

"Is my book in here, Mommy?" she asked.

"What book, honey?"

But Emma had found a picture album, dragged it out and flopped on the floor to look at it.

"What's this?" she asked innocently.

"Those are photos, sweetheart. You remember I told you about our house burning down, and we lost all our pictures and things. Our family and friends gave us copies of theirs so we could have some photos to remember."

Emma, fascinated, began to leaf through the book, pointing to each picture and asking, "Who's that?" or "What house is that?"

Alice continued to work on the boxes, glancing at each picture pointed out and responding. Suddenly Emma cried out, "Oh, there's a picture of me."

Alice felt herself go cold. "No, honey, that's a picture of your sister. Remember? I told you we lost her in the fire before you were born."

"But the girl in the picture looks like me!"

"Well, you do look a lot alike, but that's Sally. See, she is a lot older in that photo than you are."

Emma studied the picture. "She's sitting on Uncle John's lap, and there's Aunt Sylvia," Emma stated, pointing to the image in the photo.

Alice couldn't bring herself to speak. John and Sylvia both passed away shortly after Emma had been born. The child had never seen either of them, nor had she seen a picture of them before this.

"Let's go downstairs and have milk and cookies," suggested Alice, taking Emma's hand and laying the photo album aside.

Sometimes weeks went by without an "incident," as Alice began to call them. Once, as they drove near their old neighborhood, Emma simply commented, "There's my old school," and continued playing with her doll in the back seat. That night she asked about several children that Alice remembered as friends of Sally's.

"Maybe we should just move away," suggested Joe. "If she isn't around here, then she won't be…I don't know…picking up on stuff like that?"

"Do you think it's…psychic?"

"I suppose it could be. I don't know much about that stuff, but a woman in my office goes to this 'medium' who talks to dead people. I always thought it was a lot of hooey, but maybe the kid is sorta…I don't know…talking to Sally somehow?"

Alice shuddered. She couldn't envision any explanation at all that would make her feel better about this. She just wanted it to go away, and the "incidents" to stop. She was afraid moving away wasn't the answer. Besides, Joe had a very good job, and Emma was happy in her school and with her friends. All of their friends were here and what family they had left, and it didn't seem very practical to just pack up and move.

In desperation, she asked Joe to get the name of the medium that the woman in his office had gone to.

"I don't know if that is such a good idea…" Joe started to say, but Alice was insistent.

"Just tell her your wife wants to go. She won't think anything about it. People go to psychics all the time."

She was right. Carol gave Joe the name, address and phone number without question, adding that the medium was "very good." Whatever that meant.

Alice went to her appointment on a Thursday morning just after dropping Emma at school. The house was in an older neighborhood but was well kept and newly painted. Despite her expectations to the contrary, Mrs. Bailey was a sweet, middle aged, slightly overweight lady with gray hair and twinkling blue eyes. She looked like someone's grandmother, and Alice was comfortable with her immediately.

The reading began with some comments which Alice believed could apply to just about anyone.

"You've had some very traumatic things happen in your life." (So? Who hasn't?) There's a problem on your mind that has been worrying you for some time." (Big deal. Everyone has problems?) "You and your husband are both very concerned." (Her wedding band gave away the fact that she was married.) "I have a man here that comes with a fatherly feeling. Do you have a father in spirit?" (Yes, and if I say no, he will probably become a grandfather.)

"He tells me you have a daughter that you are very concerned about." (Good guess. Now take it a step further. Might as well give her something to focus on.)

"Which daughter?"

Mrs. Bailey concentrated and then frowned. "You only have one daughter."

"No, I have two, but one of my daughters passed away," Alice volunteered, but the reader looked confused and said, "No, your daughter is here among the living."

"But I have a daughter on the other side also," Alice insisted.

"No, I see no daughter in spirit. She has returned and child lives with you once again," Mrs. Bailey stated emphatically.

Oh, Lord! What was this woman saying? Emma was really Sally? Not possible, not even remotely possible!

"My dear, this is really quite unusual. Souls do not usually return so quickly. It is generally many, many years between incarnations. But I have to tell you that the child you have now is the same child you lost."

Alice stumbled to her feet, dropped two twenty-dollar bills on the table and blindly headed for the door. Mrs. Bailey took her arm gently, stopping her flight for a moment.

"Come back again when you are ready to talk about it. I think I can help you. It's called reincarnation. Unfortunately, when a soul returns so quickly, they retain much memory of the past life and this can cause some difficulties."

Difficulties! What an understatement! Alice's head was pounding by the time she reached the car; all she wanted to do was go home and lie down and forget all about this visit.

She drove home in a daze and didn't actually remember doing so when she arrived. Her stomach was churning, her vision was blurred, and she kicked off her shoes and curled up on the bed, shaking and on the verge of tears.

She immediately fell asleep, although she didn't expect to, and felt much better and considerably calmer when she awoke. The headache seemed to have disappeared completely. She picked up Emma at school, responded to her childish chatter on the way home, fixed supper, and took comfort in the mundane, common routine. After Emma was in bed, Alice sat down with Joe to fill him in on her appointment.

"Do you really believe that crap?" Joe asked incredulously.

"It makes as much sense as anything else," sighed his wife. "I want to do some research on this 'reincarnation' theory at the library, but I'm still hoping that this will just go away."

"Well," said Joe thoughtfully. "Sally only had eight years of memories, so Emma can't pull out too many more."

Then, surprisingly, the incidents stopped. Weeks went by, then months, and Alice began to breathe easier. It was over. Whatever had been happening was finished.

Until Emma made the comment about her first-grade teacher. The nightmare was back. Joe was back to pretending it was all the child's imagination. Alice didn't know how she could handle it again. Adding to her fear was the prospect of Emma reaching eight, the age Sally had been before she died. If she was really Sally, what would happen when Sally's memories stopped? Nothing in her research at the library gave her the answer to that question.

To make matters worse, Joe was leaving early the next morning on a business trip for a one-week training session in Ohio. Alice would have loved to go with him, but couldn't leave Emma with her grandmother, who would never be able to cope with her spurts of "Sally incidents." She also couldn't take the child out of school for one whole week, so she would have to stay home.

"I'm sorry, honey. When I get back, we'll find someone to help solve this problem. I have to run or I'll miss the plane." Alice kissed him goodbye and sat at the table over her coffee, waiting until it was time to get Emma up for school. Maybe she should go see Mrs. Bailey again. She needed answers and didn't know any other way to get them. She decided that it could wait for a week. After all, there had been periods when nothing strange happened before, and Joe was going to have to admit there was a real problem whether he wanted to or not and help her deal with it!

"Mommy," asked Emma at dinner that evening, "Can we go to Chuck E. Cheese for my birthday?"

"Honey, your birthday isn't for four months yet. That's a long time. We'll talk about it when it's closer."

"But I had my last seventh birthday party there, and we had a lot of fun, and I want to go there again."

Oh, Lord! Here we go again! "Let's talk about it later, Emma," said Alice desperately. "I have a headache right now."

"But I want to invite Joey and Julie and Kitty…"

"Later, Emma, we'll plan it later." Joey, Julie, Kitty…all friends of Sally's, all were at the party when she turned seven, and also at her eighth birthday party just a few days before the fire. Her head began to ache in earnest.

"Mommy, can you find my book for me? I've been lookin' for the longest time and I think I lost it."

"What book, Emma? All your books are in your room on the shelf."

"No, not the one about the little green pony. 'Member? That's my very favoritest book."

Alice thought her heart had stopped. That book had been Sally's favorite. She wanted it read to her almost every night, even after she learned to read. She could recite the whole book from memory.

"I 'member leaving my book in the car," Emma said seriously. "Last time we went on a trip, I think I forgot it. Did you find it?"

Alice had, a few weeks after the fire. It was on the floor in the back seat. In her grief, she had gathered the book and a few other things of Sally's left in the car and put them in the trash. At that point, she wanted no reminder of what she had lost.

She could feel her sanity slipping. She had to hang on. What was happening? Emma wasn't as old as Sally yet. She expected something might happen when she hit Sally's age but…then she realized. It had nothing to do with Sally's age…it was all about…when the child died. She looked up at the calendar. It was two days before the anniversary of her daughter's death…it was too late…too late to talk to Mrs. Bailey… too late to call Joe…too late for everything. Was Sally taking over Emma? Was Emma becoming Sally, or had she always been? Or was she imagining this whole thing and really truly going crazy?

Alice stumbled to the living room sofa and collapsed, holding her pounding head and crying. Emma, concerned about her mother, followed in a panic.

"I know what to do, Mommy," she cried. "They taught us all about it in school." And she ran to the phone and dialed '911.'

"My mommy needs help," said Emma. "I think her head hurts a lot and she's crying."

"Can you tell me your address, honey?" Emma carefully recited her name, her mother's name and their address, even describing the house to the operator.

She talked to the operator until she heard the sirens coming. Then she hung up the phone and climbed the stairs to her bedroom. Alice could hear nothing but a deafening roar. She was not aware when the EMTs arrived and took her vitals. She was not aware when they spoke to her and she did not respond. She was not aware when they put her on the stretcher for the ambulance.

When the EMTs were leaving, the 911 operator asked them about the little girl she had talked to.

They looked at each other. There had been no little girl. One of them headed up the stairs to see if the child was there.

And she was. Emma was sitting on her bed with her teddy bears and dolls beside her, with her arm around a big stuffed dog she called Max. She was telling her toys a story…"Once upon a time there was a little green pony…"

Guided By The Stars?

"You may find yourself in an altercation with a co-worker on Monday," Brad read. He tossed the paper down on the desk. "Why am I reading these stupid predictions?" he asked himself out loud. "What a lot of bunk."

Brad's mother was into astrology and had subjected her son to what amounted to a crash course over the weekend. Brad, a skeptic to the core, finally agreed to keep track of his horoscope during the week and report back to her on the results. In answer to his question to himself, he was reading them because his mother had extracted his solemn promise to do so…just for the week…to prove to himself that astrology worked. He agreed -- to prove to his mother that it didn't!

Brad fired up his computer and proceeded to work on the spreadsheet report due the next morning. He completed the first half before heading out for lunch.

Fred held the elevator for him.

"Hey, buddy, how's the report going?" Fred punched the button for the lobby.

"OK, I guess, "Brad answered. "There're a few figures I still am waiting for, but the rest is all done."

"Who didn't give you their info?"

"Marshall and Frank."

"Frank is always on time, but you may have to wait on Marshall's." Marshall was the slowest of the group…methodical and very accurate, but he drove everyone nuts because he checked and double checked and then checked again.

"No, he promised me on Friday that he was done with his checking and would have them to me right after lunch."

"Good luck, buddy," said Fred skeptically, as they exited the elevator and went their separate ways.

Brad grabbed a quick sandwich, stopped at the cleaners for his suit and was back in the office before one. He continued with his report, added Frank's figures, and was finally finished by 3:30, but realized that he still didn't have Marshall's info. He grabbed the phone and punched in the number.

"Marshall…Brad…you promised me the figures for the Austin report by noon. Did you forget?"

"No, but there was a change. I found an error of 14 cents and had to start all over again."

"For <u>fourteen cents</u>? Marshall, the figures are supposed to be rounded up to the nearest dollar?"

"Sorry, Brad. But I just couldn't ignore the error. I should have them down to you by the end of the day."

"Marshall, this report is due at 8 AM tomorrow. I have no intention of staying late for fourteen cents that have nothing to do with the figures. Just send them down to me now."

"Sorry, buddy. No can do. You know I take pride in being accurate in my work. I'll get them to you before 5 PM." Marshall was getting snippy and this annoyed Brad as much as the delay.

"Marshall!" Brad was shouting into the phone. "Screw the fourteen cents. I want those figures NOW!"

"When I get damn good and ready!" Marshall shouted back and slammed the phone down in Brad's ear.

Brad muttered, "Son of a ---"and slammed the phone down himself. His hands were tied. He would have to come in early in the morning to finish the report… assuming that Marshall actually did have his figures available by quitting time.

Brad headed down the hall for a meeting on an upcoming conference. It was long and boring, the speaker having a monotone voice that almost put him to sleep. When he went back to his office, Marshall's figures were in his in-basket, but it was ten minutes to five, and there was no way he was staying late. He straightened up his desk, grabbed the newspaper lying on the corner to throw it away.

"You may find yourself in an altercation with a co-worker on Monday," the horoscope prediction ran through his mind. Coincidence. Nothing more. He tossed the paper, locked his office and headed for home.

Brad made it to the office by quarter of seven the next morning, still unhappy with Marshall and his attitude, but the report would be finished before eight. He sat his coffee on the desk, tossed the newspaper on the table, and dug into the report. It took less time than he had expected and by 7:30, it was done, copied and in the President's inbox. A side trip to the break room got him a second cup of coffee and he went back to his office to relax before the rest of the crew came in at eight.

As he thumbed through the newspaper, stopping to read short articles, he remembered his promise to his mother. The horoscopes were on the Living Art page, and he skimmed down to find his "sign."

"Unexpected money will come into your hands today." Now that's one he hoped would come true. Everyone can use some unexpected money. He chuckled and tossed the paper aside.

His boss called him midmorning to praise him for the report. He had a phone call from an old buddy about a golf date that coming weekend. He finished three more reports and started a fourth. All in all, it was a very productive day.

In the middle of the afternoon, Ralph, one of his co-workers, stopped him in the hall.

"Hey, buddy, been looking all over for you. Got something for you." And he handed Brad a fifty-dollar bill, with an apology. "Sorry it took so long to pay you back. Things were rough for a while but they're a lot better now. Didn't want you to think I forgot I owed you."

Eight months ago, Ralph's wife had left him, cleaning out his bank account and taking everything in their apartment with her. The man had been in desperate shape, financially and emotionally, and Brad gave him fifty bucks to get him through until payday. He never expected to be paid back, considering it just helping out a friend…sorta like a donation to a church or charity. He had, in all honesty, totally forgotten about it. They walked down the hall together, and Brad was pleased that Ralph had gotten himself together, filed for divorce and even had a new girlfriend.

As he organized his desk before leaving the office, the newspaper again jogged his memory. "Unexpected money will come into your hands today." Well, it was certainly unexpected. Another coincidence, of course. The paper went in the wastebasket.

Wednesday was as nasty as Tuesday had been pleasant. Brad was caught in a traffic jam and was ten minutes late getting to the office. The coffee machine in the break room was broken and everyone had to get their coffee at the coffee shop downstairs—and their coffee was like colored water. The computer froze in the middle of a complicated report that Brad had not yet saved…resulting in an hour's work lost. He worked through lunch to try to catch up, but at 3:30, he went downstairs for a sandwich and coke, grabbing his unread newspaper. He needed a break, a breather, and he could hardly wait till it was time to go home. What a rotten day!

"Be prepared for a Mars-in-retrograde day. Nothing will go right for you, including the traffic. Things should be better by late afternoon."

"Should have read that damn thing before I left for work this morning," muttered Brad. "Fine lot of good that does me now. The day is almost over!" Then he had to smile at himself for taking the astrology prediction seriously. Still….three days in a row?

Thursday morning Brad took a minute to read the horoscope before getting into his car. He felt a bit foolish, but after yesterday….

"A friend may confide in you or ask for your advice. Be very careful; better to decline. If you don't, you will find yourself participating in a situation you are not comfortable with."

Well, that should be easy enough to avoid. Not that he expected anyone to ask his advice...they never do.

It was a busy but productive day. The staff meeting was shorter than normal. One report he had not been looking forward to doing was cancelled at the last minute. Coffee machine was fixed. All was right with the world, and he was looking forward to the weekend and the golf game with an old friend.

At quarter to four, Ralph came into his office and closed the door behind him. Oh, oh, that was <u>not</u> a good sign! "Can I talk to you a minute, Brad?"

"Sure, what can I do for you?"

"I need your advice. Something has come up and I'm not sure how to handle it," Ralph shuffled his feet uncomfortably.

The astrology prediction flashed across Brad's mind. Here it comes, he thought. Decline! Decline!

"My girlfriend's sister is coming to town this weekend. Shelly's a model down in New York City. Kathy and I had planned for a really nice romantic trip up to the cabin at the lake, just the two of us. What do you think I should do? Should we cancel the weekend trip? Get someone to go with us to keep her sister busy?"

It was on the tip of Brad's tongue to tell him to bring a date for the sister, but the prediction's last sentence indicated that he would end up being the date...and that was the last thing he wanted! Forewarned was forearmed. He could handle this.

"You know, I haven't a clue. I suppose you could consider a date for the sister."

"What are you doing on Sat.......?"

Before Ralph finished his sentence, Brad interrupted, "I have a golf date with an old buddy that's coming into town so I can't help you out, but good luck. Maybe Chuck would be available." Chuck was always available, especially for a good-looking girl.

"The only thing I'm really worried about," Ralph confided, "is that Kathy is so jealous of her sister. She's even afraid <u>I'm</u> going to be drooling over the girl because she's a model. She'll watch me like a hawk, and I won't even be able to be pleasant to Shelly."

Disaster diverted! He knew that if he hadn't been prepared, he would have been suckered into that date. Ralph didn't make his confession about the jealousy thing until he turned the weekend date down; "…a situation you are not comfortable with" most definitely avoided. Maybe this astrology stuff isn't so bad after all, he thought.

On Thursday night his mother called. "When can you fix this faucet for me, Brad? I really need to turn on the outside water for my plants and it leaks so bad I can't use it."

"I'll come over tomorrow night after work and fix it for you, Mom. Sorry I haven't had time to do it before. I'll pick up the stuff at the hardware store on my way over."

"Come for dinner, honey. I'll make my stuffed chicken breasts. See you tomorrow night."

She's going to ask about the horoscope, Brad thought, hanging up the phone. Do I tell her what's been happening? I really don't want to encourage her and it has got to be coincidence, anyway.

When he read Friday's horoscope, he almost choked on his coffee. "Romance is in the air. You'll find it where you least expect it." Maybe I'll fall in love with old Mrs. Wolf down at the hardware store, he said to himself, chuckling. There certainly were no eligible single females in his office to worry about. Unless his mother invited a prospective date for him—and he wouldn't put it past her – his Friday night was geared to fix the faucet, eat a good home cooked meal and make it home in time to watch the news on television at ten. If his mother invited a girl for him to meet, that didn't qualify as "where you least expect it,' so he was safe.

Brad was between girlfriends for the moment. The last relationship was a mutual parting a couple of months before. They were still friends and occasionally shared a companionable movie or dinner.

His friends could never understand how you could have a platonic relationship with a girl you had virtually lived with for six months, with no animosity, no jealousy, no emotional turmoil. He suspected his next girlfriend might have a problem with it, too, but he fully intended to remain friends with Monica. He enjoyed her company and she was fun to hang out with. She felt the same way about him. He prided himself that he always ended his romantic relationships on a friendly note.

The hardware store had exactly what he needed. Mrs. Wolf knew every inch of the store, and what every item there was used for. He suspected she could have fixed the faucet herself, if the opportunity presented itself.

It only took half an hour to repair the faucet, aided by what Brad assumed was the neighbor's little dog. Cute little thing, all hair down in its eyes and very friendly. Brad wasn't into dogs so he didn't know what kind it was, but it sure was affectionate, trying to climb on his lap and kissing his arm every chance it got.

"Are you my unexpected romance?" Brad asked the adorable pup. In reply, the dog's tail wagged even harder and it became very excited. She, corrected Brad after a quick look. "You better head for home, little girl. I'm about done here."

The puppy attacked his face with kisses when he leaned down to check the faucet. "Aren't you the little lover? Scoot on home now. I've got to go in the house."

The puppy turned and ran toward the back yard. Brad assumed she was headed back to where she belonged.

He washed up while Lila served the chicken. Table was only set for two, which was rather comforting. The subject came up over dinner, just as he knew it would.

"Did you read your horoscope this week, Brad?"

"Yes, Mom, I promised I would and I did."

"And what did you think?"

"Well, a lot of those predictions are very general. Could fit any number of people."

"Of course. There are 'any number of people' reading the column every day! They weren't just written for you, you know." His mother dished up the apple pie and added a scoop of vanilla ice cream. "But you didn't tell me if anything came true for you."

Brad took a deep breath. Might as well tell the truth. "Well… Monday I had an argument with Marshall, and it said I would have an altercation with a co-worker. Tuesday said I would get unexpected money, and a coworker paid me back a loan I never thought I'd see. Wednesday I didn't read the paper till later but it described my disastrous day to a tee. Thursday I avoided a weekend date I would have hated, thanks to the warning ahead of time."

"And what about today?"

"Well, that one was a dud. It said I would have an unexpected romantic encounter. Not very likely, since I'm headed for home when I leave here. Early golf date with Danny Plower tomorrow morning. Remember Danny? He's back in town and called me last week." If Brad hoped to steer the conversation in another direction, he was sadly mistaken.

"Yes, I remember Danny. Little short dark-haired boy with the funny ears. I supposed he is much better looking now that he's grown. So what do you think of astrology now? It was correct for the entire four days."

"I suppose there might be something to it," admitted Brad sheepishly. "I'm not about to plan my life around it."

'I'm only asking you to be open minded. I don't think that's too much to expect."

"No, Mom," muttered Brad through a mouthful of apple pie and ice cream.

His mother walked him to the door and handed him half the apple pie to take home. He gave her a hug and as he walked across the porch, a young woman with flying blonde hair came running up the steps.

"Excuse me, is Mrs. Hoffman here?" She spotted Lila in the doorway. "Mrs. Hoffman, I'm Cindy Baker across the street. I've been looking for my Shih Tzu puppy for the last hour. I don't suppose you've seen her?"

"I'm afraid not, dear. But I'll be glad to help you look. Just let me get my sweater."

"Wait a minute," said Brad. "What does this dog look like?"

"A brown and white mop," replied Cindy. "Have you seen her?"

"I think she helped me fix my mother's faucet. She ran toward for our back yard and I thought she was going home."

Cindy headed for the back yard, followed closely by Brad and his mother. There, sitting under a lilac bush, was the brown and white mop.

Cindy scooped her up, scolding her at the same time she was kissing and hugging her while the puppy squirmed in delight.

Brad had to smile at the picture they made. Cindy was a very pretty girl…well, not really a girl. He would guess she was close to 25, blonde, brown eyed with a figure that told him she worked out or exercised a lot.

"No wonder she's so affectionate," Brad commented. "She tried to kiss me to death while I was fixing Mom's outside faucet."

"Thank you so much. I was just beside myself with worry. I don't know how Peanut got out but I've been frantic. She's only eight months old. Listen, why don't you both come back to my house for coffee? It's only across the street."

"We'd love to," answered Lila for both of them, so across the street they went.

The coffee was delicious…the girl certainly knew how to make coffee! The puppy devoured her late dinner and then curled up on Brad's lap on the sofa and fell asleep.

"She certainly likes you," commented Cindy. And I like both of you, Brad thought with a smile.

Cindy had only been living in the house across the street from the Hoffman's for a week. She still wasn't settled in yet and had furniture to move around and some to move upstairs. Brad found himself volunteering to help her on Sunday, Saturday having been promised to Danny for the golf game. A little more discussion and it was arranged that Brad would come over early in the morning. Cindy was sleeping on the sofa because her bed wasn't put together yet and he could certainly get that done first thing Sunday for her.

After an hour, Lila excused herself to go back home and get the kitchen cleaned up. Brad stayed for another hour and found he really liked Cindy a lot. She had a really great sense of humor, laughed a lot, and had this great loveable puppy. They shared a lot of things in common…likes and dislikes.

"Sushi?" "Can't stand it.." "Me, neither." "Pasta?" "Love it." "Me, too."

"Sports?" "Depends on which one." "Baseball, Football?" "Yes, No." "Same here."

"Vanilla ice cream?" "On top of apple pie." "Mmmm, my favorite!"

They enjoyed the same television shows (hated reality shows, liked sitcoms) and basically only disagreed on a few things. Cindy didn't like mystery movies or Sci-Fi's; Brad wasn't fond of romance movies or the antique road show.

Brad hadn't meant to kiss her goodnight when he left, but it just sorta happened. It was nice…very nice…and he kissed her again. That was even nicer, especially because she kissed him back. After ten minutes, Brad murmured, "If I don't leave now, I might not be able to leave tonight."

"Then you better go now, because that sofa isn't big enough for both of us. Besides, we just met and I don't want you to think I'm easy."

"You are easy…easy to like, easy to get to know, and you have one very endearing quality."

"What's that?"

Brad grinned. "You have this incredible loveable puppy that looks like a mop."

They laughed as Peanut struggled in Cindy's arms to try to reach Brad. With a last promise to see them Sunday, Brad whistled as he crossed the street to his car in his mother's driveway.

On the way home, it hit him. "Romance is in the air." Well, what da ya know? If it wasn't for the fact that Peanut was really out on her own when Brad fixed the faucet, he would suspect it was a setup by his mother. Cindy was too protective of the puppy to allow the dog to roam free on the streets. The little thing was barely five pounds, for God's sake. No, Lila had nothing to do with this, much as he would like to believe she did just to prove the horoscope right.

Saturday he left the house to meet Danny before the paper was delivered, and after the game, they met some old school buddies for an evening of beer and pizza. On Sunday morning he deliberately ignored the Living Arts section, read the funnies and then headed straight for Cindy's house, stopping by his mother's first to return her pie plate.

"We really need to do a comparison chart for you and Cindy," his mother said.

"What the heck is a 'comparison chart'?" asked Brad, knowing he really should just ignore the comment, but he couldn't help himself.

"We'll do a natal chart for you and one for her," Lila explained, "drawn from the exact time and place of birth. These charts are absolutely unique and won't be duplicated for 2500 years. Your birth sign is shared by everyone who was born during those 30 or so days, but a natal chart is yours alone."

Oh, sure. That sounds logical. He always thought you were just one 'sign' and that was it.

"The natal chart comparison will tell you how compatible the two of you are and how your relationship will end up."

I already know how compatible we are, thought Brad. And who knows how any relationship will end up? This was really carrying things too far. Last week was a complete coincidence, anyway. How can the stars have any bearing on one person's life, let alone a whole group of people?

"Sure, Mom. Whatever you want to do." Let her do her thing if it makes her happy. He only promised to read his damn horoscope for one week, and that week is over.

By the time he reached Cindy's house, she had several boxes unpacked and clothes hung in her closet. Between them, they lugged the parts of the bed frame upstairs and Brad put the whole thing together in short order.

The box spring was easy, but the mattress kept sliding back a couple of steps each time they moved it up a few. It was flexible, and kept trying to fold itself, first toward Brad and then toward Cindy. They were almost weak with laughter by the time they made it to the top.

The hour job Brad anticipated actually took closer to two, and he finished adjusting the frame to the bed while Cindy fixed soup and egg salad sandwiches. They worked until midafternoon, hampered somewhat by Peanut who kept running around their feet barking for attention.

"This has been wonderful," declared Cindy. "Almost everything is in the room it's supposed to be, and I couldn't have accomplished all of this without you."

"My pleasure, milady" replied Brad, bowing low. "What do you say we take a break for a while and just go out and grab a bite to eat? Nothing fancy. Neither of us is dressed for the Chez Loraine."

"I say I'd love that. Whatever doesn't get done today I can do during the week after work."

During the next two months, Brad and Cindy dated at least twice a week. They attended a formal dinner party from Brad's work and a cocktail party from Cindy's. They saw movies, had dinner, attended a local County Fair and toured the City Zoo. They traveled downstate to visit Cindy's family on the farm and had a wonderful day.

Lila invited them to dinner one Saturday night, and after a great roast beef dinner, she presented them with their natal charts and a comparison chart.

"What are we supposed to do with these?" asked Brad.

"I'll read them for you," offered Lila. "This comparison chart will tell you how to avoid the bumps in your relationship."

"There are no bumps, Mom. Your charts can't possibly predict what will happen between Cindy and me. Just because the predictions in the paper happened to fit a few times…" He looked at his companion, who wasn't making any comment.

"Do you believe in this stuff, honey?"

"Please tell us about it, Lila." Cindy didn't answer Brad but directed her comment to his mother.

Lila sat between them on the sofa and enthusiastically pointed out what she called "aspects" in a wheel with squiggly symbols and lines all over it.

When she finished, Brad summed it up in a few sentences. "So things will be fine between us for month or two, when we will have an argument about another person, and if we both don't work to resolve it, we'll split. If we work it out, we'll have a great life together. Is that about it?"

"Well, I didn't read your charts beyond the next two years and that's really simplifying it, but, yes, that's the bottom line."

"Bunk, Mom. Sorry, but Cindy and I have met each other's friends and have no problem with them. I get along great with her family; I assume you and she like each other. Who's there to argue about?"

"The chart doesn't tell us that. I guess you'll have to just wait and see."

"Yeah, guess so." And Brad changed the subject. This astrology thing was beginning to be annoying. He hadn't been reading his horoscope in the paper and had no interest in doing so.

Their relationship grew, and blossomed into a very comfortable, loving rapport. They discussed living together, and Brad was reluctant only because his mother lived across the street.

"I would always be concerned that she would somehow …I don't know… monitor us, I guess."

"I can understand that. But your apartment is way too small, and there's no way I can bring Peanut because they don't allow dogs. Actually, you've been here more than you were there anyway and Lila hasn't been a problem."

"You're right. It will only be a problem if we let it be a problem, right? I'll move my stuff in this weekend." They discussed where to put his furniture and it seemed to work out since Cindy didn't have much to begin with. The extra bed would go in the second empty bedroom along with his dresser and clothes, since her closet was not large. Her sofa would go on the closed-in back porch and his, which was new and leather, would go in the living room.

They settled into a comfortable routine. Cindy went to work earlier and came home by three thirty. She usually had dinner ready by five when Brad arrived. Peanut was beside herself to have Brad in the house. Cindy commented that if Peanut hadn't been a dog, she might be jealous of all the attention the puppy commanded from her newest friend.

Domestic bliss was interrupted one evening when Brad got a call from Monica. She had been away in Europe for the past three months. His old phone number had been transferred to a new line at Cindy's, since many of his business associates called him at home frequently. Monica suggested they meet for dinner the next evening to catch up. He told Cindy that he wouldn't be home for dinner and why.

He explained to Cindy who Monica was, admitted they used to

live together, but emphasized that they were only platonic friends that hung out together once in a while. Cindy wasn't sure she liked that idea but his friends were her friends, so…

"I can meet you there," she suggested.

"No, you'd just be bored, honey. She's going to want to know about all our friends and stuff and probably go on and on about her trip to Europe." Cindy just raised her eyebrows and didn't say a word. "I won't be late."

But he was. By midnight, Cindy was restless and couldn't get to sleep. By one o'clock, she was hoping he hadn't been in an accident or anything; by two she was beginning to get angry. How dare he stay out this late with another woman…especially one he used to sleep with! He didn't come home until close to 3:30 in the morning. He had obviously had several drinks, which didn't help matters any. What kind of a patsy did he think she was!

It was not a pleasant scene, and Brad ended up in the extra room bed for the rest of the night, which was only an hour or two before Cindy had to go to work. She was gone by the time Brad dragged himself out of bed, showered and forced himself to go to the office. He didn't see what Cindy was so upset about. Monica was only a friend, for God's sake, more like a sister than anything else. They got to talking and forgot about the time. Was that a crime? He wasn't going to let a woman run his life, even one he loved as much as he did Cindy.

He left work early because his head was aching rather badly. Those last three drinks were really not a good idea, he decided, but Monica was on a roll, telling about her adventures in Italy and it was impolite to let her drink alone.

Cindy was already home, had given Peanut a bath and had supper started. At least she wasn't so mad she wasn't going to feed him, he thought wryly.

"Brad, I think we need to talk about this. I don't think that was very considerate of you to spend the night with an old girlfriend, especially when you refused to let me come, and said you would not be late. Think about it. What if I had spent the evening with an old flame and came home half sloshed at 3:30 in the morning? How would you feel?"

Brad had the grace to look sheepish. Deep down he knew he hadn't been fair to Cindy. He was putting a strain on their relationship and it had nothing to do with Monica. If he had done the same with Danny, for instance, she probably would not have been quite as upset, but it still would not have been very considerate. Either he was committed to this relationship with Cindy, or he wasn't.

"I don't suppose you want to hear this," continued Cindy, "but your mother warned us about this situation when she did those charts, remember? Now we can either resolve it…or not. The end result is up to you. I'm willing to work on resolving it. I love you and want us to continue to be together. I guess it all depends on what you want."

Brad took a deep breath. "I want us to be together, too. Monica is just a friend, but certainly not as important as you or our relationship. I won't see her again, if that is what you want."

"Heavens, no! I'm not trying to run your life or tell you who you can be friends with. All I ask is that you don't shut me out. Do you think I would like Monica?"

"I think you would. She's really a good person and you'd get along with her just fine. She isn't the jealous type…certainly doesn't want me back, if that's what you are worried about. In fact, she met a man in Italy that wants her to come back there and marry him. She talked about him for most of the night, and I think she's making up her mind to do it. Hope she'll be happy…he sounds like a great guy."

"Then we have nothing more to discuss. Let's kiss and make up. That's the only good part of arguing," Cindy laughed, as she threw herself in Brad's arms.

After dinner, Cindy brought up the astrology issue again.

"Do we tell your mother she was right about the comparison chart?

"Naw," replied Brad, "Don't encourage her. You know that horoscope stuff is just a lot of bunk."

Spaced Out

"All I know is," said Marcia," he has really weird eyes."

The other two girls at the table, Carol and Sandy, both raised their eyebrows without comment. They knew who Marcia was referring to, and both thought that his eyes were not the only weird thing about Jason Kelp.

Jason had been present at a community dance that all three girls had attended the previous evening. He was polite and soft spoken, and really didn't do anything out of the ordinary, but there was just something about him…something in his aura…that wasn't quite… right. He had seated himself next to them at the table and focused his attention on Marcia, who had at first been flattered. After all, Jason was a good-looking man…too handsome, perhaps…with almost perfect features, golden curls and brown…no, hazel…no, green…eyes. As Marcia observed, he had weird eyes which seemed to be a different color every time you looked at him. Still, he hadn't done anything that you could fault him for…he was unfailingly courteous, complimentary and a gentleman to the core. Perhaps that was the problem…he was just too perfect.

"He smiles at the right time, but it doesn't reach his eyes," observed Sandy thoughtfully. Carol nodded in agreement as her friend continued.

"It made me nervous that when he looked at me; he seemed to see right through me…like he knew everything I was thinking. I never met a man that actually <u>looked</u> at me like that!"

"Well," said Carol, "we probably won't see him again anyway. That wouldn't hurt my feelings any. He really makes me nervous."

"Unfortunately, I will," sighed Marcia. "Mr. Norris just hired him. He's going to be working out of our office."

You poor thing!" said Sandy. "When did that happen?"

"This morning, I guess. Mr. Norris took him around introducing him just before lunchtime. Jason acted like he'd never met me before, which I thought was a little strange. The funny thing is…he almost made <u>me</u> believe he hadn't!"

The conversation came to a close when Carol and Sandy, with a glance at their watches, grabbed their dishes in preparation for leaving the cafeteria and returning to their office, which was one floor above Marcia's.

Marcia had a longer lunch break but had to go to the post office on the bottom floor of their building before returning to work. They separated at the elevators, reaffirming their plans to meet after work for a shopping trip and dinner.

Over dinner, Marcia reported that Jason had not been around the rest of the day, so the subject was not mentioned again the rest of the evening.

Marcia was pleasantly tired after their shopping trip and more than ready to go home. Carol dropped her off at the apartment building where Marcia had a comfortable two-bedroom place on the second floor. The apartment was stuffy from being closed up all day, as she had forgotten to leave the windows open as she usually did. She immediately opened the French doors onto the patio, pulling the drapes back.

Her apartment was modern but very homey, with a cushy brown leather sofa, bright flowered drapes, and a deep pile carpet in beige and green tweed. Kicking off her high heeled sandals, she padded barefoot into the bedroom, shedding her suit jacket and blouse, and tossing them on the bed. She was completely undressed and headed for a nice long shower when the phone rang. Hesitating for only a moment, she continued into the bathroom, letting the answering machine take the call.

She was ready for bed before she remembered the phone had rung earlier. The light was blinking on the machine and she pushed the Play button.

"Marcia. This is Jason Kelp. I'd like to see you this weekend if you have no other plans. Please call me at 761-5855."

Shaking her head, she pushed the Erase button and crawled into bed. She was not the least bit interested in seeing <u>him</u>. Besides making her a rather nervous, he acted really strange…not even acknowledging that he had met her before when Mr. Norris introduced them. She also wondered where he had gotten her phone number, until she remembered that her boss had assigned him to the HR department.

She spent Saturday morning cleaning her apartment and making potato salad for a picnic at her mother's the following day. Grocery shopping only took an hour in the afternoon and she picked up a couple of videos at Blockbuster to watch that night. She thought maybe she would invite Carol or Sandy to come over and watch them with her. Then she remembered that Carol had a date and Sandy said she was driving out to see her folks in the next county for the weekend.

When Marcia arrived home from the store, the light was blinking on her machine again. She pushed Play as she passed by to drop the grocery bag off in the kitchen.

"Marcia. This is Jason Kelp. I'd like to see you this weekend if you have no other plans. Please call me at 761-5855."

Good heavens, it was the identical message. She knew she had erased the previous one, but it seemed to be exactly the same. Again the Erase button wiped the tape clean. She decided she would have to screen her calls or next time she might answer and have to actually talk to him. She jumped as the phone rang again, but the caller ID showed her mother's number.

"Marcia, dear, you are planning to come for the picnic tomorrow, aren't you?"

"Yes, of course, Mother. I have the potato salad all made."

"Good. Be here by one, if you can. Oh, and Marcia, bring your suit. The pool was just cleaned and it's supposed to be really hot tomorrow."

The movie she chose was boring…so boring, in fact, that she fell asleep in the middle. She woke briefly around midnight and used the remote to shut off the TV but went right back to sleep.

Marcia was up early the next morning, having fallen asleep earlier than usual. She was able to get her laundry done, clean her apartment and visit the local library before it was time to go to the picnic. The morning was, as promised, very warm, and by noon the temperature was in the 90's, a perfect day for swimming. She packed the potato salad in the cooler with ice packs, grabbed her swimsuit and left her apartment just after twelve.

It was a half hour drive to her mother's house and she wasn't surprised to find she was the last to arrive. An invitation to a Johnson picnic was highly desirable in the small town where she lived, and everyone invited always showed up, usually early. Fortunately, the back yard was almost half an acre, especially since the crowd generally numbered in the forties.

The elaborate house was an old, converted inn and had a large parking area on the side. She maneuvered her little Saturn into an empty end spot where she could hopefully get out early if she wanted to without being blocked in, well aware that these gatherings often went on into the wee hours of the morning.

Camille was, as usual, enjoying her role as hostess. She greeted Marcia enthusiastically, handed the potato salad to a maid hovering nearby, and hooked her arm in her daughter's, prepared to introduce her to anyone she didn't already know. There were only three new people…a college professor from the nearby University and the new owner of the hardware store down the street and his wife. People were already in the pool and Marcia excused herself to change into her suit. She wasn't feeling particularly sociable and swimming was a good way to avoid being drawn into a conversation.

As she re-entered the pool area, towel over her shoulder, Camille waved her over to meet someone she was talking with. Reluctantly Marcia complied and was surprised when the man turned and smiled at her. What on earth was Jason Kelp doing at her mother's picnic?

Before she could say she already knew him, her mother had introduced him and he solemnly took her hand, saying, 'I'm pleased to meet you, Marcia. Your mother has told me so much about you." He was acting as if he had never met her...again! Just like at the office when her boss introduced them! No reference to the fact that he worked in her office; no reference to the two phone messages left on her machine. Camille flashed them a smile and excused herself to continue her hostess duties.

"Okay, what's going on?" Marcia demanded. "Are you stalking me? How did you end up getting an invitation to my mother's picnic?"

"Camille was kind enough to invite me when we met last week. Is there a reason I shouldn't be here?" he said, curiously.

"I have no control over who she invites to these affairs," Marcia responded testily.

"You don't like me, do you?" asked Jason, calmly. He didn't seem upset or angry, just mildly inquisitive.

"I don't know you well enough to have an opinion." Marcia was rather embarrassed and was sure she was blushing. She was usually not judgmental about anyone, but Jason Kelp made her very tense and uncomfortable. She still couldn't put her finger on why.

"If you'll excuse me, I would like to take a swim before lunch." She walked away quickly and plunged into the pool, swimming quickly to the far end, as far away from Jason as she could get.

She managed to avoid him the rest of the afternoon, but every time she saw him, he was looking straight at her. By early evening, she made her excuses to her mother and headed for the parking lot. Dismayed, she saw her car was blocked in by another vehicle. In a chilling burst of intuition, she knew the car belonged to Jason Kelp! It made sense since he was the last to arrive after she did.

She weighed her options. She could call a cab, but that would mean an explanation to her mother as well as another cab ride back to get her car tomorrow. She could borrow her mother's car, which was on the other side of the house in the garage, which would mean an explaining that to her mother also. Or she could ask Jason to move his car so she could leave.

Logic told her the third option was probably the only one that made sense, so biting her lip, she returned to the pool area, first noting the make of the car and the license plate, hoping she was wrong about the owner.

She located him chatting with the college professor, and taking a deep breath, walked up to him and said, politely but firmly, "Would you mind moving your car so I can leave?"

"Of course," he said instantly, and excused himself to the professor. This confirmed what she suspected...that he knew it was her car he had blocked in. She forced herself to walk calmly beside him to the parking lot.

"Are you sure you want to leave so early?" he asked.

"Yes, I have things to do," she replied. Her tone of voice said clearly it was none of his business, but he asked anyway.

"What things?"

"Nothing for you to be concerned about." It was a polite way of saying 'none of your business.'

'I'm not concerned, but I would be very interested. I'm trying to learn everything I can about life here."

"You mean life in a small town?"

"No, I mean life here...how people think, what they do, what motivates them."

"Are you some kind of psychology professor?" She asked. They had reached the parking lot and she unlocked her car.

"You might say that," Jason said. "Listen, I'm on a ...mission, and I could use your help. It's very confidential, but I believe I can trust you to be discrete and not discuss it with anyone. Could we meet somewhere for coffee and talk about it?"

"I suppose," she agreed reluctantly. She was more curious than anything else at this point. Maybe she could get to the bottom of the mystery...why he seemed so different and why he made Carol and Sandy, and herself, so nervous.

He backed out and allowed her to take the lead, following closely behind her. A few miles down the road was a diner and she turned in and parked, Jason parking in the spot next to her.

They took the booth in the very back and after ordering the coffee, she waited patiently for Jason to start explaining what he wanted from her.

"Marcia, I come from a place that is...far away from here. We live a lot like you do, but there are differences that we would like to...change. What I am here to do is learn about those differences."

"I don't understand," she said, confused. "We aren't any different than anyone else. What kind of differences are you talking about?"

Jason was silent for a moment. Finally he said, "Emotions. I'm talking about emotions. You people laugh, you cry, you feel things that we don't. You get angry, you get sad, you get happy...I need to find out how and why."

"My goodness," she laughed nervously. "You sound like you are from another planet!"

He just sat quietly, not responding or reacting to her comment.

Marcia gasped, her face losing its color. "Is that it?" she blurted out. "Another planet? My God!"

Still no response...no denial or confirmation, but she didn't need it. She knew.

"Why did you pick me to confide in?" she asked shakily. "What makes you think I can help you?"

"I know you...feel things. I know you believe, unlike a lot of your people, that there is life on other planets. I know you've been interested in UFOs since you were a child."

"How do you know that? I never told anyone I....saw one except my mother, and she didn't believe me. In fact, I'm not sure I believe it myself now. I was only a child. Maybe it was my imagination..."

"No, it wasn't. We mean no harm, Marcia. We just want to learn, to make our life better and more interesting. You can help us do that."

"Do you think being able to feel sad or guilt or unhappiness will make your life better? It won't; it will only complicate it. Stay the way you are. That's my best advice."

"But you have to know sadness before you appreciate joy, and you have to know unhappiness before you can feel happiness. Our lives are shallow, we need depth, and emotion will give us that depth."

"It will also give you more problems than you want. "

Jason leaned his elbows on the table and looked at her closely. "Why do you care?"

"I don't know…I just do. I know what it's like to be unhappy. I know what it's like to be sad. I wouldn't wish that on anyone, especially on a whole planet of people who don't have to deal with it."

"But you would be helping us. We really want to learn."

"Jason, emotions are nothing you can learn. You have to experience them. There are no books or classes or exercises that I know of that will teach you how to feel emotions. I can't help you or your people. I wouldn't even know how to start."

Then I have failed in my mission. I will just continue to observe until it is time for me to return to my home. Perhaps I will be able to learn enough to give us some direction. I would ask you to keep my confidence and not discuss our conversation with anyone."

"You have my word. No one would believe me, anyway," she replied. "Good luck," she added, as she stood up to leave.

"I'll see you in the office tomorrow," said Jason, making no move to leave with her.

She couldn't have told anyone how she got home because her mind was spinning so much she simply didn't remember the drive. Before she knew it, she was back in her apartment getting ready for bed. No, she couldn't tell anyone…not her mother…not her friends…they would all think she had totally lost it. He seemed harmless enough without any bad intentions. Better to let Jason do his observing and then leave when he was supposed to. She did not…absolutely did not…intend to get involved in his "mission."

On the other hand, maybe he was really not from another planet. Maybe he was delusional. Not necessarily a threat to anyone, but just whacked out. She sighed and wished she could believe that theory. Unfortunately, she suspected he was exactly what he said…from out there in space. Half the books in her bookcase dealt with UFOs, alternate universe theories, space travel. Her friends thought she had some rather kooky beliefs but had no idea how deeply she had delved into the subjects. Apparently Jason somehow did know which was rather scary.

She dreaded seeing him in the office on Monday, but he acted like he always did…like he didn't know her. He nodded good morning in the hallway and kept walking. Marcia was relieved. Sooner or later, he would be gone, and things would be back to normal.

Then she started thinking about the books in her library, her lifelong interest in the subjects, and realized that she had been too hasty. Here was a marvelous opportunity to actually be in contact with and learn about someone from another planet! Maybe she should reconsider…if he really wanted to learn about emotions, she could probably help… at least on a clinical level. Learning about them was one thing, feeling them another. But that was his problem, not hers. Meanwhile, she would learn all she could about his planet and his people.

Before she changed her mind, she sent him a quick email. "Have reconsidered. If you still want my help, you have it." The response was back in minutes… "I'll call you tonight." She grinned to herself. It was almost like he had been waiting in front of the computer, expecting her message. Well…. maybe he had. She had a lot to learn about Jason Kelp and his people.

He called, and they arranged to meet at her apartment the following evening right after work. He arrived bearing a large pizza piled with meat, mushrooms and extra cheese.

"That wasn't necessary, Jason," said Marcia, as she opened the door and invited him in.

"I have observed that bringing the meal is the proper thing to do when calling at the dinner hour," he stated. "And I find this particular dish very pleasing. We have nothing like this at home."

"You see, you're already learning. Finding pizza pleasing means you like it, and 'like' is an emotion."

"Hmm," he said, obviously considering her comments. "Yes, I do… like it. Our food at home is simply for nourishment and one neither likes nor dislikes it. It just is and we partake to survive."

"Then you already have something to take home with you," she observed, biting into a slice of the hot, gooey pizza and enjoying every mouthful. From the look on his face, Jason was also enjoying it, the first step in the right direction. Maybe this would be easier than she thought. Perhaps part of the problem with his planet was that there was nothing available to enjoy, or hate, or love.

"Tell me about life at home, Jason," she asked, curling up on the sofa with a second slice.

"We live very simply," he began, also helping himself to another piece of pizza. "We do not have three meals a day, as you do. We intake food twice a day, morning and evening, and it is the same every day. It is called tolofa, and contains everything we need to sustain life. Our hydration is from sonobal, a liquid that also provides life sustaining qualities. There is no taste, but it gives us the moisture our bodies need and we intake it also twice a day."

"Do you sleep on your planet? Where do you live?"

"Yes, we rest for several hours a day to rejuvenate our bodies. We also visit a crystal cave on a regular schedule which rejuvenates us. My home is very much like yours, in a tall building. But all buildings look alike, all living spaces are alike. I have what I need…a room and bed for resting, a place to store the tolofa and sonobal. You have here one thing in your living spaces we lack. We have no color…only gray and black and white. I find color very interesting… very enjoyable. Perhaps we need color in our living spaces also."

"Do you have growing things? Like plants and trees?"

"Yes, but they aren't green like yours. We do not have…flowers. All plants have a purpose; some are used to make the tolofa and sonobal. The trees provide the oxygen we need to breathe. They also provide the building material for our living and working spaces."

"How do you move about? Do you have cars? Busses? Trains?"

"We have spoken enough about my home, Marcia. Let us talk more about yours. I am here to learn more about your people. I know all the answers about your environment to the questions you asked about my planet. I am here to learn about feelings and emotions, if you remember."

'Yes, of course. Well…it sounds like you are lacking in things you can have strong feelings <u>about.</u> People here have more things they can… feel about. Our food, drink, homes and so forth. Even colors…people like or dislike colors, sometimes say they love certain ones or hate others. I don't think it's as much a problem of not being able to feel emotions as not having any stimulation to generate feelings," Marcia observed, finishing her slice of pizza. "Now how about a cup of coffee?"

"Does coffee sustain life?" Jason asked curiously.

Marcia laughed. "Some people think it does, especially in the morning when they first wake up. No, it doesn't sustain life, but if you like the taste, you drink it because you like it. Or it makes you feel good or gives you energy. Not everything has to be for a life sustaining purpose. In fact," she mused," very few things here on earth are. Perhaps we should take some lessons from your people."

The more they talked, the more relaxed Marcia became. She actually began to enjoy being with Jason. Surprisingly enough, she found he even had a sense of humor…an odd one, to be sure, but a sense of humor nevertheless. She turned on the TV (Jason said they didn't have such a thing) and caught a few minutes of the Jerry Springer show. Jason was aghast at the screaming and fighting going on between the guests. She assured him that she believed it was all make-believe and rehearsed, but he could not comprehend why anyone would be waste time watching people out of control, especially if it was not even real. Marcia had to agree, since it was not her idea of entertainment.

She flipped to the Animal Planet station where someone was feeding and petting several dogs. Jason asked what purpose dogs had, and she had to admit that they were mostly just companions to man, and something to love, a concept he had trouble grasping. There were no pets on his planet. Or love either, apparently.

After he left, Marcia sat on her bed in her pajamas and recorded the information she learned from Jason in a notebook. She realized she had forgotten to ask what his planet was called or exactly where it was in relation to earth, but they had another session planned for the next evening and she made a list of questions to ask him then.

She turned down an invitation to go to a movie with Carol and Sandy, who stopped by her office on Friday morning, and she admitted rather reluctantly that she had an appointment with Jason and couldn't go with them.

"You're <u>dating</u> him?" asked Carol incredulously.

"Not exactly," said Marcia, "We just…share information…talk…you know."

"No, we don't know," answered Sandy for both of them. "What kind of information?"

'Well….Jason needs…some tutoring, and I agreed to help him on the subjects I know a lot about."

"Sounds rather fishy to me," said Sandy and Carol nodded.

"Nothing fishy about it. We are just <u>working</u>, nothing more. He really is very nice…not weird like we thought at all. But honestly, there's no romance or anything like that going on."

"What kind of subjects?" persisted Sandy

"Mr. Norris asked me to work with Jason, "said Marcia, desperately pulling the lie out of thin air.

"Well, if your boss asked you…" said Carol reluctantly, but Sandy wasn't buying it. She put both hands on the front of the desk and leaned over, her eyes locked on Marcia's.

"What could you possibly know that Mr. Norris couldn't tell Jason himself?"

The phone started ringing, and Marcia said quickly, "I have to take that. We'll get together soon. I promise." Reluctantly, Carol and Sandy left her to her phone call.

"So was my timing good?" asked the voice on the phone. Marcia laughed. It was Jason, and he apparently knew what he interrupted.

"Perfect!" she answered. "I don't know how you did that, but you saved me from an interrogation I would not have been able to avoid."

"Could we try Chinese food tonight?" Jason asked. "It has so much color I think it must have a very interesting taste."

"Sure. I'll order a variety and have it delivered. Do you like… Never mind. I'll just pick out something." Sometimes she forgot Jason had no idea what he would like. Whatever she ordered would be a new experience for him, and another step in his education.

They were making progress. He found he liked broccoli and didn't like peaches. When she asked what the tolofa tasted like, he replied,

"Nothing at all. There is no taste, no flavor, no color. You only ingest the assigned amount for its nutritional and life sustaining value.

"When I first was sent here to learn about feelings and emotions, I did not realize that it encompassed many things…like other people, and food and entertainment. Your whole society is based on it. I do not think I can ever learn enough to bring our people up to your standards."

"You don't have to, Jason. Once you bring color and different foods to your home, your people will automatically change. They can't help but either like or dislike what you have brought. Either way, it will be an emotional experience for them."

The one thing Jason wanted to experience, since he saw it on television, was a kiss. Reluctantly, Marcia agreed to let him kiss her.

Jason put his arms around her and just stood quietly for awhile, gently rubbing her back. This is nice, thought Marcia. Very non-threatening and very comforting. He must have been very observant when he watched that TV program. Finally, he bent and gently touched her mouth with his.

It was like no other kiss she had ever experienced, almost like an electric shock went through her body. His lips were warm and moist and gentle. As he deepened the kiss, her mouth opened automatically and before she knew it, she was experiencing the most erotic kiss of her life. When he finally let her go, her head was reeling and her knees were weak.

"Most pleasant and most enlightening," murmured Jason, his eyes changing from hazel to very dark blue. And he kissed her again.

Reluctantly she pushed him away. There was only so far she would go to educate him, and if she didn't stop…

There was a subtle change in their relationship after that. Jason kissed her good night each time he left after their meeting, and while it was very enjoyable and often very passionate, neither of them allowed the situation to go any further. Sometimes he held her hand and squeezed it while they talked. Sometimes she had trouble concentrating on what they were discussing, and she had to keep reminding herself that this was not someone she could have a relationship of any kind with! He was from another planet, for heaven's sake, and was only here temporarily. Getting involved was simply not an option.

After two weeks of sessions virtually every night, Marcia had still not made much progress on her notebook. She knew the name of his planet and had a vague idea of where it was located, how he arrived on earth and how he would leave when it was time. There didn't seem to be much else to know…everything was identical, everything was colorless and…well, boring. They had a leader that made decisions which were accepted by all without protest, not that there were many decisions to make.

Life went on day after day with nothing of interest happening. Jason himself was absorbing information about earth like a sponge and his personality was developing by leaps and bounds. Fortunately, Carol and Sandy had accepted her explanation that Mr. Norris had asked her work privately with Jason and hadn't bothered her, outside of a raised eyebrow or two when they occasionally passed in the hall.

Finally he announced one evening that this was their last session. He was being returned to his planet and had gathered what he needed to make some changes. His small apartment was filled with seeds, books, samples of paints, foods…whatever he could transport. Marcia had a few more questions and Jason promised to answer them if he could. She realized that in all of their conversations, he had never answered any personal questions.

"You've never talked about your family, Jason. Are you…married?"

"There is no marriage or relationships on our planet like on yours, so no, I am not, nor do I have parents as you do. I'm totally alone."

"That must be difficult for you. If there are no marriages, then what about children?" Marcia asked

"Children? What children?"

"You do have children there, don't you?"

"No, no children. Only adults. We were created fully grown in the laboratory. Once the population reached a certain point, no new people were created. Our planet is rather small and cannot sustain more people than we have."

"What happens when someone dies?"

"No one dies, as they do on your planet. We remain as we are until we can no longer function. Only then is a new one created to replace the old."

"And what happens to the old?" Marcia asked reluctantly. She wasn't sure she wanted to know.

"Recycled, of course."

"Recycled how?"

"You recycle on your planet. I have heard all about organ transplants and using body parts when people no longer need them. It is basically the same as on ours."

Marcia suddenly had a strange feeling that she had been missing something vital all this time. When Jason said he was created in a laboratory, she had a quick vision of something similar to in vitro fertilization, but that didn't explain a full-grown adult from a lab. Perhaps she wasn't asking the right questions, or maybe she didn't want to know the answers!

"Uh… what 'parts' do you recycle?"

"All parts, of course, unless the computer chips have been damaged somehow. These are the only parts that cannot be recycled and must be created new. If the chips must be replaced, then the person is considered 'new.' When something wears out or stops functioning, we are given another part, which may be either recycled or new," he explained. It seemed very important to Marcia that she understood, so he wanted to be as clear and explicit as possible.

"Jason…are you…human…or a…robot?"

His brow furrowed. "Neither human nor robot, as you know on your planet," he said seriously. "We are far more advanced. We used your human specifications as our physical model and we only needed the emotions I have learned here to be complete. My mission was more successful than anyone could expect, thanks to you, Marcia."

Stunned, Marcia stared at him. He <u>looked</u> human, he talked and acted human and he certainly kissed like a human. Oh God! She had been making out with a <u>robot</u>!

"Human specifications? You mean you are…exactly like us physically?"

"Exactly! Our planet has both male and female," he confirmed, an actual twinkle in his hazel eyes. "Anatomically correct, I believe is the term you use."

Then she could have…they could have…Thank God they didn't!

Jason hugged her one last time, kissed her quickly on the cheek, and then he was gone. Marcia stood in a state of shock in the doorway, watching him jog down the stairs, whistling.

This was not the same mechanically polite Jason that she first met at the community dance. This was a jubilant Jason who had feelings, emotions, and opinions, who liked broccoli and hated peaches, who enjoyed experiencing new things, who kissed like a dream and who had taught her just as much as he had learned himself.

And apparently was a very high-tech robot!

The bottom line was…Marcia would really miss him. And considering how he had developed on earth, she suspected he would miss her, too.

Of course, that wouldn't make any sense to anyone else, not that it mattered. Because she couldn't tell a soul, anyway.

Printer Magic

"Darn thing's acting up again!" muttered Katie, pulling off a sheet of gibberish from the computer printer.

It only happened sporadically, but it always seemed to be when Katie was printing out a letter to her boyfriend. Ralph was at a six-week training conference in California, and Katie tried to write him nearly every day. The printer always worked fine for everything else, but the letters she wrote him never seemed to print correctly. Her best friend's husband, who worked on computers, mentioned something about a print driver, but couldn't explain why the darn thing worked just fine the rest of the time. Katie used her notebook computer constantly for work, and she never had a problem with the printer on those occasions.

However, strange things would happen with the letters to Ralph; sometimes entire paragraphs would just be missing; sometimes half the words would be misspelled, and they were correct on the computer screen, and sometimes, like this one, there was nothing but gibberish and odd symbols on the whole page.

"I suppose I could just actually write him a letter with a pen," Katie said out loud to her cat. Herman lifted his head and looked at her. Katie liked to talk to herself, but always felt foolish. It was a bit more acceptable, she thought, to talk to the cat, even if the cat didn't really care or respond. Her handwriting was atrocious, and she knew it.

"He could probably make more sense out of this stupid page than if I tried to hand write it," she murmured, tossing the useless letter in the wastebasket. Later. She'd do it later.

Katie padded in her stocking feet to the refrigerator for milk and then pulled up a chair to climb up and pull a package of cookies off the top shelf of the cabinet. At barely five feet tall, she couldn't reach the top shelf without standing on something. It had been a brilliant idea to hide cookies and other goodies too high to reach, but unfortunately, her sweet tooth would win out and she always gave into temptation. Katie was pushing 120 pounds, too much for her small frame, but she could never seem to resist chocolate chip cookies.

She pulled her long blonde hair back and fastened it out of the way with a rubber band, grabbed her milk and bag of cookies, and flopped on the sofa in front of the TV. The phone rang before she could even dunk the first cookie.

"Put the cookies back, Katie," said a sweet voice on the other end. Darn…how did her sister know? Must be something to this "twin" thing.

"Leave me alone, Karen, it's been a long day and I deserve something."

"What you don't deserve, honey, is a few more pounds. Now put the cookies away. You can have the milk."

Grumbling, Katie pushed the cookies to the center of the coffee table and settled back for a chat with her twin sister. Katie and Karen were fraternal twins but looked a lot alike. Both had long honey blonde hair, big blue eyes, a cute little nose…except that Karen was five foot four and had a figure to die for. She always claimed Katie wasn't overweight, just too short!

"Have you heard from Mr. Wonderful?" asked Karen. She did not particularly like Ralph but confined herself to a snide remark every once in a while. She believed Katie would learn soon enough what kind of guy she was dating.

"He's been real busy at the conference," Katie replied. "I'm sure he'll call me this weekend."

"Hmmm," was the only response from Karen, and she changed the subject.

"Are you planning to go to Mom and Dad's for dinner Sunday?"

"I guess so. I'm volunteering at the Center on Saturday, but Sunday is free."

After a few more minutes of conversation, Karen had to leave to pick up her daughter at day care.

At 27, Karen had already been married five years and had a darling little four-year-old girl. Her husband was a local businessman; they had a house with a pool and two cars. She was a contented housewife, ideally happy and felt completely blessed.

Katie, on the other hand, was an auditor for a large insurance company, sometimes worked far too many hours, had had two very unsatisfying relationships and was intensely serious about this one, even though she suspected deep in her heart that this was another bummer, despite his profound claims about loving her. Truth be told, she hadn't heard from Ralph in three days, and he couldn't be THAT busy. California was full of pretty girls, girls a lot skinnier than Katie! She sometimes wondered just what Ralph saw in her, as he was very good looking and had women fawning over him all the time. To give him credit, though, when he was with Katie, he totally ignored all other woman. Except now he wasn't with Katie....

Katie had three days off in a row and was at rather loose ends. None of the businesses she was auditing were open for the holiday on Monday. She was already caught up on all her audits and they had been turned in. She didn't know exactly what she was going to do with herself for three days with Ralph gone. Once again she tried to print out the letter to Ralph, and once again it was just a bunch of symbols and a few letters thrown in. She studied the paper intently and then looked again. If she ignored the symbols and just put the letters together, it spelled out

GOTOCALIFORNIA.

How freaky! She pulled the other letter out of the wastebasket and sure enough, the same symbols and letters appeared, and it too spelled out the same thing.

Surely there was a message there, thought Katie. Fate, or something. Impulsively, she called the airlines and made a reservation on the next flight to Los Angeles, which left in just under two hours. Katie packed a bag quickly, put down plenty of food and water for Herman and gave Karen a quick call. There was no answer, but she left a message on the machine…

'Karen, please check on Herman. I'm off to California for the weekend."

The cab got her to the airport in plenty of time to pick up the ticket and catch the plane. Once in her seat, she took a deep breath and wondered if she should be doing this. Maybe she should have called Ralph first…he could be very busy this weekend with work for the conference …or maybe it would be better to just surprise him. If he had appointments, she could find something interesting to do and surely he couldn't be tied up every evening!

It was a short flight, just over an hour, and Katie caught the shuttle bus for the hotel where Ralph was staying. As she approached the front desk, she overheard the desk clerk telling the woman ahead of her that the hotel was full and there were no available rooms. "Not a problem," thought Karen and smiled sweetly at the clerk.

"My husband has our room key. May I have another, please?"

"Name?"

"Ralph Wilson, Jr."

The clerk shoved a paper at her and said, "Sign here." Quickly she scribbled "Mrs. Ralph Wilson," picked up the room key card and left.

The number on the card was 2252. Riding up in the elevator, she had second thoughts again. Maybe this wasn't such a good idea. Would Ralph be mad because she came? Of course not, it would be a grand surprise! The elevator stopped on the 22nd floor and the doors opened. Karen stepped out and found 2252. The card was inserted and the door opened.

As she expected, the room was empty. But what she had not expected was a tube of bright red lipstick on the dresser, a pair of nylon pantyhose draped over the chair and a slinky black nightgown on the bed. Hurt and angry, she was tempted to just leave and go back home on the next plane. But Ralph deserved more than that. He deserved a lesson!

Gathering up the articles, she stuffed them in the nearest drawer. She replaced them with her own nightgown, a pair of her own pantyhose (which were considerably shorter than the others) and a tube of her pink lipstick. Then she hid her small suitcase in the bathroom and settled down to wait.

Some two hours later she heard voices in the hall and turned off the light, slipping quickly into the bathroom.

Ralph and the girl came through the door, giggling and talking. Katie knew the exact moment when the girl spotted the strange red nightgown, the short pantyhose, and the bright pink lipstick. The giggles turned into screaming obscenities, with a totally confused Ralph unable to even grasp the situation, let alone try to come up with an explanation.

Katie waited until she heard the final scream, the sound of a slap across a face, and a slammed door. There was dead silence, and then Ralph hollered in frustration, "What the hell just happened?"

At that point Katie walked out of the bathroom. Ralph was sitting on the foot of the bed shaking his head. Before he could register surprise at seeing her, she grabbed her belongings and said "You just got caught, Ralph," gave his other cheek a resounding slap, and left the room, slamming the door behind her.

On the way to the airport, she started to giggle as she remembered the scene in the hotel. She wondered if she would ever hear from Ralph again…and hoped she wouldn't. She had to wonder about the message on the printer. Where did it come from, and why? It was the only reason she came to California, and if she had not, who knows how many more times he would have cheated on her?

Katie was able to catch the last flight out of Los Angeles and arrived home around midnight. She should have been depressed, but for some reason, she was rather elated. The cookies still sat on the coffee table and she put them back on the shelf, not even being tempted. Herman didn't seem to know she had even been gone, but then she worked so many hours he was used to being alone.

The two jumbled papers lay on the desk where she had left them. Idly she picked them up and put them in the desk drawer. She wanted to show Karen when she told her about her quick trip. Then she went off to bed with a strange feeling of contentment…like something good was just around the corner.

Ralph never called, apparently too embarrassed at getting caught, or maybe he just didn't care. Katie went on with her life as usual, and the printer worked perfectly when she worked on her audits, or typed notes to her parents or former school friends.

She met Karen at their parent's for Sunday dinner and both her parents and sister were rather relieved that Ralph was history. Although nobody had ever actually said anything to her before, she learned that none of them trusted him and all had a bad feeling about the man from day one.

"I wish you had said something," Katie complained.

"Would you have listened? No, of course you wouldn't. We don't want to interfere in your life, honey, but we do worry about you and want only the best for you." Her mother patted her hand, while Karen rolled her eyes in the background.

She didn't tell her parents, or Karen, why she decided to fly to California that night, but two weeks later Karen stopped by one evening. Katie told her the strange story and handed her the papers. Her sister studied both sheets, puzzled, and said, "I don't see what you are talking about. Where does it say 'go to California.'?"

"Put the letters together," directed Katie. "What does it spell?"

"G C T P G F L I E B M N I C," read Karen.

"What?" Katie exclaimed and grabbed the paper. The letters were there, exactly as Karen had read them aloud. "OK, what's going on? It clearly spelled out GO TO CALIFORNIA. What happened to the letters? Now I'm really freaked out! This is just too weird!"

"Whatever is going on, it saved you from another scumbag. Don't question it!"

"That's it, then. I'm swearing off men…for good. My luck with the opposite sex simply sucks!"

The next few weeks Katie felt better than she had in ages. She credited the change in weather…she always felt better when it was sunny and warm. Her audits went smoothly, even the large difficult ones. Life was good…a little lonely…but good.

One afternoon she was plugging figures into the program for an audit, and the screen suddenly went blank.

"Oh, no," said Katie to her cat. "Now what!" Herman never stirred. Apparently he had no idea either.

The screen came back on, the audit intact and she breathed a sigh of relief. Until she went to print the spreadsheet.

Symbols and letters…just like before. She whacked the printer with her hand, not expecting it to help, but it made her feel better. Print cue again…again jumbled information. The audit was due to be mailed that afternoon. Maybe she could save it on a disc and take it to Kinko's or someplace to have it printed.

Curiously she looked at one of the sheets with the symbols and letters. If she ignored the symbols and just took the letters….

"No, I'm not doing that again!" She said aloud. But she was. She couldn't help herself. Quickly she jotted down the letters and then divided them into words.

"TAKE ME TO GRESHAMS," it read. Greshams? That big computer place on Main Street? Well, maybe the computer was smarter than she was. Maybe the computer knew who could fix this problem.

Remembering what she went through with Karen before, she carefully circled each letter on the paper. Yes, it actually did say "take me to Greshams." OK. Greshams it was. She grabbed the paper to show the repair person what the printer or computer was doing.

She stood inside the door for several minutes, feeling a bit foolish. The place was packed. She could be waiting for hours for help.

From across the store, a young man looked up from his desk, stood and came directly toward Katie. She watched him as he approached, and he looked one step classier than the rest of the clerks…nice suit and tie, good looking with a wide welcoming grin.

"Could I be of help to you?" he asked. Katie smiled. He had a slight English accent…a definite plus. She loved accents.

"I seem to have a strange problem with my computer and it told me to bring it here."

To his credit, the man didn't bat an eye. "Then let's see what needs to be done to take care of this problem," he said with a smile, and led her to the back corner to his desk.

A flustered young clerk came hurrying up. "Mr. Norris, I'll take care of that." Mr. Norris waved him off and plugged in the notebook.

"I'm Alex Norris, the manager here," he said as he pushed the power button. "I don't often get a chance to actually work on computers anymore, but today is extra busy and I need the practice."

"Just how did your computer direct you here?" he asked curiously.

Katie blushed. This was going to sound really, really stupid. "I printed out an audit, and it came out with nothing but symbols and letters, and the letters spelled out 'take me to Greshams.'" Now he would think she was some kind of nut! She handed him the paper.

He studied it seriously for a few minutes and then said gravely, 'Well, then, I would say you came to the place you were supposed to." No smirk, no funny look, just totally serious. Katie let out the breath she didn't know she had been holding. She wasn't crazy. The computer actually did send her here!

He booted up the notebook and began typing. To Katie, it looked about as readable as the printed scrambled page, but he seemed to understand the information on the screen. Alex continued to type, faster than she had ever seen anyone type before, and apparently continued to get information from the computer. She just stood back and watched, studying the man concentrating on the computer screen. He was not very tall, but then he was about the right height for Katie; brown curly hair—one lock kept falling over his forehead and Katie itched to push it back--really penetrating blue eyes. And that accent…

"There," he said finally. "I think that should do it. You had a virus…not one of the bad ones that wipe out your system. Just one of the annoying little bugs that act up every so often."

"Thank you so much," said Katie, relieved. "What do I owe you?"

"I should think going to dinner with me would take care of it." He smiled. "Would you?"

Katie hesitated. Did she dare? She had sworn off men. But this one was so nice!

"I'll give you lots of references," Alex said. "My whole crew here at Greshams will vouch for me. I've been manager here for three years, my mother lives on Highland Street and my brother is an attorney with Langham and Langham law firm. I've never been married and I'm 28 years old and very healthy. What else do you want to know?"

Katie laughed. "I guess that should do it for now. Yes, I'll have dinner with you. There's only one problem. I have to print out and mail the audit I was working on today."

"No problem." In a few seconds, Alex had her notebook hooked up to a printer. "Go ahead." It only took a few minutes to print the audit, and it printed correctly. Alex gave her a large envelope and she stuffed in the audit, addressed it and pulled out a priority mail stamp from her purse. Alex took the envelope from her, said "we have a post office run once a day," and handed the envelope to one of the clerks. Then he picked up the computer, took Katie by the arm and escorted her through the front door.

"How can you just leave your job? Isn't it too early?" Katie asked.

Alex leaned over and whispered in her ear. "I'll tell you the truth, "he said softly. "I'm also part owner, so I can play hooky if I want to."

It was too early for dinner, so they went to the lake in the park and rented a rowboat. Katie had no problem talking to Alex, and they shared childhood stories and high school stories and compared teenage life in England with life in the US. Alex had a delightful sense of humor and kept Katie laughing most of the time. They had an early dinner at a small French restaurant and then walked on the beach by the lake and shared their dreams for the future, touching briefly on mistakes and failed relationships in the past.

Katie finally realized how late it was. They had been together for eight hours straight. Alex took her back to her car in Greshams' parking lot and then followed her home to be sure she was safe.

He walked Katie to the door, kissed her goodnight and promised to call the next day. Katie was walking on air, but there was still that tiny doubt. Would he really call? Would she see him again? Would this one work out? She had picked three duds before; how could she trust herself this time?

They dated for the next three months. He met Katie's family and his family met Katie. Her parents and sister professed to like him, but then they didn't tell her the truth with Ralph so she couldn't be sure. His mother was very nice and seemed to like her, but how could she tell? Alex was very attentive when they were together, but then Ralph had been also. Would Alex like her better if she were skinny like her sister? Lack of self-confidence is a horrible thing, she decided.

Katie was cleaning out her desk and organizing her files one morning when she came across one of the scrambled pages from the second problem with the computer. She smiled as she looked at the paper...this was what brought her to Greshams and Alex. Idly she picked out the letters to see the message again, and with a feeling of horror, realized that the combination of letters spelled...nothing at all. It was a repeat of the California fiasco when Karen showed her the message didn't exist!

She backed away from her computer as if it had suddenly grown horns. What was going on? She had shown Alex the paper when she brought the computer in the first time. He must have thought she was crazy when she told him she saw the message. Or maybe he thought she had a vision problem! Katie groaned aloud. Herman just looked at her and curled up in the sun on the window seat again. When she got up the nerve, she would ask Alex about it. Maybe he saw the message, too. Maybe...

It never seemed to be the right time to bring the subject up, although it was constantly at the back of her mind, taunting her. One afternoon Katie was fixing dinner for Alex in her apartment. Alex was upgrading some software on her notebook computer. After dinner, while he watched TV and rubbed Herman's stomach, Katie booted up the computer to print out the audit she had done that morning. The screen went blank, then came back and the page printed came out in symbols and letters, just like before. Katie's heart sank. Not again! Well, at least she had someone to fix it this time. She picked up the paper and scanned the letters.

"I wonder what this message says," she said jokingly, and couldn't stop herself from writing down the letters in the order they appeared scattered across the page.

WILLYOUMARRYME

She turned to see Alex leaning on the door jam, smiling.

"Well, will you?" he asked. Her doubts flew out the window, as Katie flew across the room and into his arms.

On The Wild Side

"With my luck, it's probably poison ivy," Cara muttered, trying to ignore the tingling itching sensation on the back of her legs. She carefully moved out of the patch of brush onto the path, looking for a convenient low branch of a tree to pull herself up and out of the way of whoever or whatever might come along.

"I wish I was ten again," she sighed, as it took more than one attempt to swing up onto the branch and scramble up the tree a few more feet. Once settled in the crook of the old oak, she managed to examine her legs to find only scratches instead of the poison ivy blisters she expected. Maneuvering her small backpack from her shoulders to her lap, she opened the zipper and took out the aloe vera gel that she carried with her on her excursions. It was soothing, and she leaned back against the trunk with another sigh. Now if the fates would just cooperate and send her what she was looking for, she could head for home and a nice long hot bath.

Fate being fickle, she spent the better part of two hours perched in the tree to no avail. When the shadows of the woods told her the sun was about to set, she shimmied down, picked up the bundle she had left at the base of the tree, and trotted down the path toward her pickup truck parked in a clearing several yards away.

She wasn't prepared for the huge missile that came from behind, knocking her flat. Panicked, she tried to throw the weight off her back, but a low growl in her ear stopped her cold.

"Just don't move and you won't get hurt,"

Cara froze. The object was obviously a man...a large bear of a man, and she was alone and unprotected on someone else's property. Suddenly her expedition didn't seem like the good idea it had when she conceived it earlier that day.

"You're trespassing on my land. What do you think you are going to find?"

Again the low growl in her ear sent chills up her spine.

"If you let me up," she said shakily, "I'll tell you."

Instantly the weight was removed and she took a deep breath before getting to her feet and turning around to face her attacker.

He was big, but not as big as she imagined when she was face down on the ground. She expected a much older man, since the owner of the property was close to sixty, but this dark-haired man couldn't have been much over thirty, and he would have been very good looking except for the scar across one cheek. Oddly, that didn't detract from his looks but only added some mystery. If she had to guess, she would have said he was August Sandborn's son, Mason, although no one had heard from him for over ten years. He and his father had a violent disagreement and Mason had simply disappeared.

"Well, when you've done checking me out, you might answer my question," he demanded.

"My name is Cara Edwards and I live three miles over across the stream," Cara explained carefully. "My cat has wanderlust and I've been tracking him for two days. I think he is probably somewhere on your property."

"A cat? What kind of cat?"

"Well ...actually he is a bit bigger than a cat...more like a...cougar." She winced as the man's face lost its color. Of course he would think a cougar had to be a wild dangerous animal and feared for his livestock and animals. Skeeter had never attacked an animal in his short life, but this man would never believe that.

"Skeeter is…a house pet. He really is only a baby and wouldn't hurt anyone or anything."

"Listen, lady. A cougar is a wild animal…I wouldn't trust one as far as I could see him. In fact, I would just as soon take my rifle…"

"No! That's what I was afraid of! That's why I have been trying to find him before he gets hurt! Please…he really wouldn't hurt a fly!"

"You better hope he won't. If he attacks anything on my property, he's history! Maybe you better stop sneaking around and just find the beast."

"I was trying when you tackled me, "Cara said indignantly. "I brought his supper in this bag and I was hoping I could entice him to come and eat, and then I would have taken him home without anyone being the wiser."

'You can stay out here all night, as far as I'm concerned. Just find him and do it fast!" The man turned on his heel and stalked off up the path in the direction of the house, which she knew was almost five miles away. She supposed he had a horse over the rise, since she hadn't heard any engines, and noisy four-wheelers were the only type of vehicle that the land would accommodate.

Cara breathed a sigh of relief. Now that she didn't have to sneak around, she could call the little brat.

"Skeeter! Skeeter! Get yourself over to me right now!" Immediately the little cougar trotted out of the woods, surprising even Cara. Apparently he had been there all along, just hiding from his mistress, and then was probably afraid to come out when Mason (she was assuming that's who he was) came along. At least she had proof positive that Skeeter wasn't dangerous. He didn't even come out of hiding to protect her when she was mowed down by the angry owner!

"Bad kitty. You should be punished for running off like that!" Cara scolded. She picked up the bag, ignoring Skeeter's pitiful look as his supper disappeared into her backpack. Then she continued to scold him as she scooped up the animal, but was rubbing his ears at the same time, much to his delight.

After Skeeter was safely ensconced in his room, supper in the dish and fresh water nearby, Cara flopped down on the sofa. She knew she had to make a decision soon about the cat. She had been postponing bringing him in to the Wildlife Rehab Center, but now that someone else knew about the cat, she would have to do something and do it soon.

Cara had been on an herb finding trip in the mountains when she came across the tiny animal all by itself in the woods. She never knew what happened to the mother or to the other cubs, if there were any, but Cara couldn't leave the helpless kitten alone in the woods. Actually, she had been surprised to discover there were even cougars in the area. She had gotten a wildlife report from the State before she moved into the area, and cougars, also known as mountain lions, were not even mentioned. It was late in October, a substantial snowstorm was predicted, and she was reluctant to leave her home for fear of being trapped in town for the winter. She called the State Wildlife Department, and was told that their facility was, for the moment, much too full. David, the inspector, was also surprised that she had found a cougar cub and confirmed that there had been no reports of the animal in the area. He suggested that she take care of the baby until the weather broke and she could bring him in and turn him over to the preserve.

This wasn't exactly protocol but since her father had been a wildlife rehabilitator and had worked for the Department several years ago, Dave was willing to waive some red tape. He had known Cara since she was a little girl and knew there were always wildlife babies in their home for days and sometimes weeks or months, depending on the situation. Although her father has passed away years ago, Dave had confidence in Cara's ability to care for the cub until spring.

Cara brought the cub home and fed him formula made with canned milk from a baby bottle for a few days until she decided he was old enough for solid food. Before the winter was over, his blue eyes had changed, and his spotted coat was becoming a more even tawny color, so she estimated that he was about seven months old—old enough to go wandering and get himself in deep trouble but too young to be out on his own. Cubs usually remain with their mother until they are a year old, and often longer, learning how to survive on their own. Cara was very attached to the affectionate cat, and besides being too young, Skeeter was too humanized at this point to send him back to the mountains to fend for himself. He had no idea he wasn't a person and would get himself shot the first time he came in contact with another human.

When he finished eating, Skeeter trotted into the living room and jumped up on Cara. She pushed him off to the side, telling him he was getting too big to hold on her lap but hugged and cuddled him as he curled up beside her. They watched TV together... Skeeter liked the Animal Planet station…and Cara absently scratched his head between his ears while he purred so loudly he almost drowned out the sound on the TV.

'I'm not ready to give you up yet," she whispered into his fur. "But you simply can't go wandering onto the Sandborn property. I know you need space to run and I'll do my best to find someplace safe for you until we can get you down the mountain to the Rehab Center." What Cara was actually hoping was that she could convince Dave to recommend that she be allowed to adopt the cat. There was a great deal of expense, red tape, and politics to having an exotic animal as a pet, but Skeeter was worth it. Her property in the hills of the backside of nowhere was large enough as she owned ten square miles. An inheritance from a grandfather she never knew came at just the right time in her life, when a bad relationship turned even more sour and she was ready to abandon her entire lifestyle for peace and quiet.

Being so far from civilization suited Cara perfectly. The closest neighbor was August Sandborn, and she had only seen the old man once. He was very reclusive and not very friendly. Usually neighbors depended on one another for survival, so when Cara made the forty-mile trip to the nearest town for winter supplies last autumn, she stopped at the Sandborn place to ask if she could get anything for him. He was extremely rude, responding by saying "Mind your own business" and slammed the door in her face. She could almost feel sorry for the son if he was back there with his father.

When Cara first arrived to check out her inheritance a year ago in March, she was rather surprised to find a comfortably large log cabin, a barn and two other outbuildings situated in a clearing. Apparently her grandfather was very self-sufficient, with an old but working generator as well as a windmill-powered electrical unit. The well water was clear and pure; the barn had obviously been unoccupied for several years but needed very little repair.

The house had two bedrooms, a large kitchen with a wood range for cooking and a pantry (Cara had always wanted a pantry), a large stone fireplace in the living room and—wonder of wonders—and indoor bathroom connected to a septic tank. The shower was the greatest luxury. A propane powered water heater was small but heated enough for dishes and a shower once a day. It was a struggle for Cara to wrestle the tanks into the truck to take them for refill, and she reasoned that her grandfather must have been extremely strong for his age! Fortunately, three tanks lasted several months and once she figured out how to switch the lines, all she had to do was keep the two extra tanks full and on hand.

She quit her job, sold her flat and almost everything in it, bought a new four-wheel drive pickup, and arrived one spring morning in April with nothing but her clothes, a TV set, a bed and a truck full of supplies. The lawyers had told her that her grandfather had made most of the furniture himself. Crude but serviceable...a table and four chairs, two bed frames with feather bed mattresses, a nightstand or two and a surprisingly comfortable but very ugly sofa and chair. There was no TV reception, so Cara installed a dish which worked sporadically, depending on the weather. She wasn't sure she installed it right, but it did work occasionally and the signal seemed to be better at night, which suited her just fine.

Her phone service was reduced to her cell phone, which only worked in one particular spot near the house, so calls during inclement weather were not possible. Still, it was a very comfortable place to be, and certainly provided the peace and quiet she craved. She had hoped it was early enough in the year for a garden, and she spent many pleasant days digging the plot and planting seeds and plants she obtained on one of her rare trips into the nearest town. The beans were growing very nicely when a family of rabbits came by one morning and in seconds, stripped every new plant to the ground and then disappeared. The next day she made a special trip to pick up fencing and she had no problem after that.

Cara found some interesting items in one of the outbuildings. In a battered trunk were several old cookbooks, apparently belonging to her grandmother, which gave her information on how to can vegetables from her garden. Three cases of fruit jars in the corner of the shed were dragged inside and carefully washed. The sealing lids were too old and dried out to use so she had to buy new ones, but she gleefully canned her garden produce at the end of the summer and smiled each time she opened a jar of tomatoes or pickles. Her biggest challenge was learning to use the wood range, but after months of practice, she felt she did a passable job. It was a wonderful feeling…being self-sufficient and knowing it.

Other books in the truck were valuable resources from which she learned about the herbs for healing and for seasoning. Markings in the margins gave indications as to which could be found in the nearby woods. It was on one of these forays that she came across the cougar kitten.

Since it was now early May again, Cara was thankful that the winter was over. It had been long, cold, and snowy, and many days she never ventured from the cabin. Skeeter went outside for brief periods to take care of his needs but was happy to return inside to the warmth of the fireplace…that is, until this last trip when she had to go looking for him. The snow was fortunately melted, trees were bursting with new leaves and she had already planted her garden.

Skeeter had not been happy to be locked in the barn while she made a trip into town for supplies and plants for her garden, but she couldn't take him with her and certainly couldn't leave him alone to roam. Truthfully, she should have taken him to the Wildlife Rehab Center, of course, and Dave probably expected her any day, but she wasn't ready to give Skeeter up yet and since her cell didn't work well enough, Dave couldn't call her.

"Maybe he forgot I have the cub," she thought hopefully, steering the truck down the rutted path that passed for a road. Skeeter was again locked in the barn and had cried pitifully when she left. She had no choice as her propane was dangerously low.

At the hardware store, she let the yard workers take the tanks to be filled while she went inside. Maybe there was some kind of enclosure she could buy to keep Skeeter safe but still allow him some freedom… an invisible fence, perhaps?

She was studying the brochures taped to the shelf when she heard an unwelcome but familiar voice.

"Well, if it isn't the cat lady."

Cara lifted her head up slowly and stared at Mason Sandborn. He didn't look quite so big or quite so menacing in the store, but he still was far from friendly.

"So is the beast roaming around outside on my property today?" He asked rather sarcastically.

"No, he's safely locked away. I wouldn't <u>dream</u> of exposing my pet to the dangers of wandering onto your land."

"Well, well, the lady has claws like her cat," he said with a grin that was anything but friendly.

"That's right," Cara responded. "And if you're smart, you'll leave <u>both</u> of us alone!" She grabbed the brochure from the shelf and stalked down the aisle in the opposite direction, making her way to the counter to pay for her propane.

"Odious man," she muttered. "I probably forgot everything I came in here to get!"

She wondered if she should stop by and talk to Dave, maybe approach him on the adoption of Skeeter and get the paperwork started. No, she better just call him from home. She didn't want to get involved with any of the other employees in the office sticking their "two cents worth" in and encouraging Dave to deny her.

She stopped at the store to buy several gallons of ice cream. The weather would soon be too warm for her favorite dessert to survive the long trip home, even in the thermos cooler. She had the forethought to buy a small freezer last fall since she liked frozen vegetables even better than home canned ones and needed more space for meat than the small freezer on the refrigerator. There was plenty of space left in the new freezer for at least six gallons. Another few pounds of hamburger would come in handy also. Skeeter's appetite was increasing by leaps and bounds. She wondered how long her nest egg would last at this rate!

At the last minute, she remembered she planned to buy a harness and leash. He would probably outgrow it soon, but it would give her a chance to train him to stick with her and he wouldn't be able to take off on his own. Skeeter was about 30 pounds and fortunately small enough yet that she could control him.

She left town early to avoid being caught in the dark on the road. The first twenty-five miles or so were blacktop and no problem; the next fifteen were gravel road, which still bore some of the ravages of winter but was passable if she was careful to avoid the bigger potholes. The last five miles were barely a wide space between the trees and it was a stretch of the imagination to call it a road. If she was lucky, she would navigate those miles in just under half an hour. The "road" was a right-of-way through the corner of the Sandborn property and she hoped she wouldn't run into its latest resident as she crept by.

With a sigh of relief, she pulled up next to the cabin and hurried to the barn to let Skeeter out. He was obviously annoyed with her, and stalked by with his head held high, refusing to look at her. Cara had to chuckle because he so resembled an incensed male human.

Skeeter headed directly for the cabin and Cara let him in. She hadn't thawed out the hamburger before she left, so she used some of the fresh meat she had just gotten from town. Skeeter ate, and then settled onto the sofa for their nightly ritual of TV and ear scratching. Apparently, he wasn't annoyed enough to forego that pleasure.

Cara and Skeeter were both ready to abandon the TV for bed when a pounding on her door startled her. Skeeter looked confused and then disappeared into his room. Heart pounding, Cara reluctantly went to the door. She reasoned that a burglar or anyone planning to do her harm would not knock. There were no locks on the doors as her grandfather obviously saw no need.

She flung open the door and was not surprised to see her tormenter standing there glaring at her.

"What exactly is your problem?" She couldn't help but yell the words.

"It's not <u>my</u> problem. It's <u>yours</u>, lady." The angry man retorted. "Your damn animal killed one of my dogs."

"And just when did this massacre take place?" Cara asked coolly.

"Late this afternoon," was the answer. "I found Rex behind the barn all torn up."

"First of all, Skeeter is too small to do much 'tearing up," she retorted. "Second, he was never trained by his mother to hunt or kill, and third, as I told you in the store, he was locked in my barn all day while I was in town.

"Since he hasn't learned to unlock doors as yet," she continued sarcastically, "and since he was still there when I came home, there is no way he could be guilty. Look for your perpetrator somewhere else!"

The big man just stared at her. Cara started to slam the door in his face, but he stuck his foot out and blocked the door.

"Look, if your cat didn't do this, then someone or something else did, and that means we <u>both </u>have a problem."

"No, <u>you</u> have a problem. "Cara again attempted to close the door.

"No, the problem belongs to both of us. If there is something in this area that is killing animals, yours are just as much at risk as mine. You didn't see what was left of my dog. I don't suppose you want to take a chance with that beast of yours being attacked."

"Of course not," Cara hesitated, sighed and opened the door to let him come inside.

"I guess I should introduce myself," he said, shutting the door behind him. "I'm Mason Sandborn, August's son."

"I know...that is, I assumed you were the first time you attacked me."

He had the grace to look a bit ashamed. "Sorry about that. I guess we got off to a pretty bad start. I've been back a couple of months, and found my father in real bad shape...the doctor said he has a very bad heart and needs constant monitoring, and I had to find a place for him to be taken care of.

"Actually," he continued, sitting down in the chair Cara offered to him. "Rex isn't the first animal that was killed...mutilated, actually.

Since I've been back, we've lost two cats and one newborn calf, all the same way. I have to admit I'm not convinced it is an animal doing this."

Cara shuttered. If not an animal, then…what? A person? Who would do such a thing?

"When I saw you sneaking around in the woods, I thought… well…I thought maybe,"

"You thought I would do such a thing?" Cara's eyebrows rose.

"Not after you explained who you were…well, I almost was hoping it was your wild cat."

"Cougar," Cara corrected automatically. "So how do we go about finding out exactly what…or who…is doing this, and stop it?"

"I don't know yet," Mason said grimly, "but if it's a person, there has to be a reason…and it probably involves money. Just about everything in the world does." He finished with a grin. "Do you have a phone here?"

"Only a cell phone, and that only works in one or two spots. I think the mountains cut off the signal or something."

"Our cabins are too far apart for any other kind of signal. I guess for now we'll have to wing it. Just be really careful, whether it's dark or light out. That doesn't seem to matter. Do you have a gun? "

"Lord, no! I wouldn't know how to fire one and I'm sure if this is a person, he could take a gun away from me much easier than I could shoot him."

Mason stood up to leave. He was reluctant to leave his horse alone out behind the cabin for very long, and it was now totally dark out. He would have to trust the animal could find its way home. It had been too many years since he roamed these woods and wasn't really sure how to get back to his father's cabin on his own.

They parted on a friendly note, but the conversation left Cara rather nervous. She had never been afraid to be alone in the cabin, but she was suddenly very aware that there were no locks on the doors. Not that it mattered that far out in the country. Locks never actually kept anyone out…just made it more difficult to get in. Who would hear her if she screamed for help? Maybe she should buy a large fierce dog for protection. Skeeter certainly wasn't a threat to anyone, unless he licked them to death!

Needless to say, Cara didn't have a very restful night. After a few days with no sign of trouble, she began to relax. Maybe Mason was being paranoid. Could have been a coyote that got his animals. Except that she knew that a coyote would have not just mutilated an animal and left them there. Still, there was nothing more happening and nothing she could do at this point.

Mason got in the habit of dropping by at least once a week to check on how things were going. Cara shared her vegetables from the garden with him, fed him lunch a couple of times, dinner three times, and even Skeeter lost his shyness and seemed to enjoy his company. Mason treated the cougar like he was just another cat, scratched his ears and rubbed his belly when Skeeter threw himself on the floor at his feet and flipped on his back.

Skeeter outgrew his harness and Cara couldn't find one in town big enough. She estimated he weighed in at 50 pounds and was too heavy to carry around. He was really too big to control, but he seemed very docile around Cara and did as he was told.

They rambled through the woods frequently during the day while Cara gathered wild mushrooms and herbs. She felt that the presence of the cat would discourage anyone who might think about doing her harm. Skeeter seemed to stay close to her and not wander off, for which she was thankful. Nothing was forthcoming from Dave, although she managed to avoid him when she went to town, and she began to believe that he was just going to ignore the fact that she had a cougar...illegal as it was..

Summer was in full swing; her garden promised to out produce the year before and she was looking forward to a freezer and pantry full of food for the coming winter. At her request, Mason bought more canning jars and lids, as she promised to use her overabundance of vegetables to provide some winter supplies for him also.

Cara rescued an old sewing machine from one of the sheds...her grandmother's, most likely. Mason worked on it for several afternoons and finally it was able to produce a passable stitch. Delighted, Cara made curtains from flowered sheets she found in the closet. The hitherto masculine flavor of the house became quite feminine with the addition of her decorations.

The lazy summer days came to an abrupt halt late one afternoon when Mason came to her cabin on his four-wheeler.

"Hi...I didn't expect to see you today," called Cara from the shed she was turning into a chicken house.

"Didn't expect to be here," replied Mason shortly. "Where's Skeeter?"

"Just across the field. I just saw him go into the woods a minute ago, why?"

"Call him in," he said grimly. "We've had another massacre."

"Oh no!" Cara exclaimed. "Surely you don't think Skeeter..."

"I think Skeeter would be safer here than out in the woods right now." Mason replied, "And no, I don't think he had anything to do with it."

Cara called several times before they saw the big cat bounding from the woods and across the field. Cara was actually a bit surprised when she observed his size. She really hadn't paid that much attention, but now she was aware that Skeeter was no longer the playful kitten she used to have. Practically full grown, he was probably at least seventy pounds, muscular and all signs of his spotted coat had long since turned to solid cinnamon and nutmeg colors. A quick calculation and she realized that he was probably close to a year old.

"Skeeter, stay close to the house now," she admonished and he flopped down beside her after nudging Mason with his head in a familiar greeting.

"Mason, what did you find?" she asked, not sure she even wanted to know.

"I don't know if I told you, but I found a stray puppy when I came back from town Friday. Brought him home. Guess someone had dumped him by the side of the road. Anyway, he was in the woods behind the house this morning, along with one of the yearling calves.'

She shuddered. "I don't want to know any details," she said.

"Cara, I don't think it's safe for you to stay here alone."

Her chin came up and she looked him in the eye. "Nobody...and I mean nobody...is going to drive me off my land."

"Spoken like a true pioneer woman," Mason smiled, "but not very practical. If I could just find out why someone wants us freaked out enough to leave…"

"Ask your father," suggested Cara.

"What does he have to do with this? He isn't even living here anymore."

"Yes, but maybe…just maybe someone tried to buy the land or get him to move before this. He would know if there was a good reason that somebody wants you, or even us, gone."

Mason promised to visit his father in the nursing home the next day.

Cara woke to find Skeeter standing over her, one big paw on each side of her body. He was making strange growling noises, and for a moment, she felt a stab of fear.

"Skeeter, what do you think you are doing?" She made herself sound authoritative and fearless.

Skeeter again let out a low growl, leaped off the bed and padded toward the door. In the doorway he stopped and looked at Cara and again let out another growl.

Cara soon realized he wanted her to follow him, quickly threw on her jeans and sweatshirt, grabbed her cell phone automatically, and then patted his back.

"OK, fella, where to?"

Skeeter bounded toward the back door and when she opened it, he headed for the road. Cara grabbed her keys, leaped into the truck and started it. Skeeter trotted down the road and then stopped and waited for her. Soon they were creeping along the rutted path, Skeeter in the lead and staying back so Cara could follow. Instinctively, she left only the running lights on. It seemed to take forever to navigate the three miles to the Sandborn driveway. Skeeter stopped and then headed into the woods beside the road.

"Wait," called Cara. She abandoned the pickup just past the driveway and jumped out to follow the cougar. It actually seemed faster on foot as Skeeter led her toward the house.

At the edge of the clearing, she saw the lights on in the house. There were no curtains and what she saw through the open window nearly caused her heart to stop. Mason was tied to a chair and a large man with a knife was standing facing him with his back to the window. Cara couldn't see his face, but when he turned his head, she realized he had some sort of hood or mask over his head.

Cara found her cell phone and prayed there was a signal where she was standing. No luck. She tried moving a little closer to the house and out into the clearing. Still no signal.

She knew she would not be able to guarantee a signal until she was halfway to town, and she was not about to leave Mason in that situation for that long.

"What can we do, Skeeter?" she whispered to the big cat. Skeeter dropped to his belly and began slinking along the ground toward the house.

"Skeeter, come back," Cara couldn't call out except in a hoarse whisper. Skeeter ignored her. "Get back here," she demanded in a whisper. Skeeter continued to slink across the yard. Finally, as Cara watched helplessly, he stood and began to run toward the open window.

The man inside raised his arm with the knife in a threatening gesture toward Mason. Skeeter, with a mighty roar, sailed through the open window, landing on the man's back, and began roaring and growling. Terrified, the would-be assailant dropped the knife and tried to crawl toward the door, only to be pinned to the floor by seventy pounds of extremely angry cougar! The man screamed as Cara came through the door, "Get this beast off me!"

"Be quiet and he won't hurt you," she ordered, "but move or try to get up and you'll be his favorite lunch!" No option there. The man cowered on the floor, whimpering, and made no attempt to get up or to reach for the knife.

Cara quickly confiscated the knife and used it to cut Mason free. Skeeter stood over the man prone on the floor, emitting periodic and very fierce sounding growls.

Mason used the ham radio on his desk to contact the police. Then he found a length of rope and used it to tie the assailant's hands and feet while Skeeter stood by...just in case. Once the man was trussed up like a Thanksgiving turkey and his mask pulled off, Skeeter quietly jumped out the window and disappeared into the woods.

"Smart cat, "whispered Mason. "I'm sure you don't want to explain a cougar to the officers when they come."

Cara smiled. She was certain Skeeter would be waiting for her when she got home. Meanwhile, all they had to do was deny anything the would-be assailant claimed about a huge beast attacking him.

It took the better part of an hour before the police arrived. Mason had time to fill Cara in on the situation.

The man was Robert Spencer, who represented the owner of a lumbering company that had been trying to buy the Sandborn land for the past year from August. Their offer was ridiculously low, but they thought that since August had no heirs (Mason had been missing for years) and probably had no idea of the value of the land anyway, he would sell out easily.

However, August had refused their offer, so they tried to frighten or coerce him into selling, figuring they would have no problem with the lone female next door. The company had lost some prime logging land in the next county and was facing bankruptcy if they couldn't scare August and then Cara into giving up their land. They started with killing the animals to scare the old man but hadn't counted on Mason moving in and August moving out. Spencer was threatening Mason, hoping to find out where the owner was so they could force him to sign the property over to them.

When the police arrived, Spencer began babbling about a mountain lion attacking him. The officer took Cara and Mason aside to ask them exactly what happened and what was this about a mountain lion?

"I suppose this guy is just embarrassed because he was taken down by a mere woman," Cara explained. "Yes, I do have a cat...a house pet, and he was with me when I came to see Mason, but I can't imagine anyone being threatened by my little kitten. Does this man look like he was attacked? Any scratch or bite marks? My kitty doesn't even catch mice, let alone attack six-foot men!"

The officer had to admit there was no physical evidence that he had been attacked by a wild animal, or even a tame one. There were also no other reports of cougars or mountain lions in that area of the state, so Spencer's story didn't even make sense. While the man now in custody continued to babble about this huge mountain lion and describe his experience in graphic detail, the officer quietly made out his report, indicating that Cara had surprised and subdued the attacker, who was apparently delusional. Mason backed up her story so that was the report that went down officially. The Sandborn land was only one piece of property they were trying to obtain in various underhanded and illegal manners, and the police had been keeping an eye on Spencer and his boss for quite some time.

It was after midnight when Cara arrived home. Skeeter was lying on the front porch waiting. He let Cara rub his ears and then trotted off into the woods. She realized that she no longer had a kitten on her hands, and Skeeter was now in charge of his own fate. Cougars are nocturnal by nature, and he knew where the borders of her land lay. As long as he stayed on her land, he would be safe. Cara would continue to feed him when necessary and let him stay with her when he wanted company. Skeeter in turn would protect Cara and her property (and Mason's, too) from any threats, two or four legged.

She would never know how a lone cougar cub came to be abandoned in the woods on her land, but as long as Skeeter was around, she would never worry about being safe.

Time Will Tell

Jaime was late. This was not an unusual occurrence...in fact, for her, it was quite normal. Jamie had, for some reason, an aversion to time...clocks, watches... anything that marked the passage of time. She felt it was controlling her life and apparently she subconsciously resented it and rebelled. Even when she was younger, her poor mother struggled daily to keep her from missing her school bus. Fortunately, as an adult, she found a job that didn't require a strict schedule. She wandered in anywhere between nine and ten but worked extra hours frequently. Her boss didn't seem to have a problem with that, as Jaime was an excellent worker and her performance - once she arrived - was faultless.

Unfortunately for Jaime, there were things that happened in a specific time frame...planes, for instance. Airlines were rather picky regarding having their passengers at the airport and on the plane in a timely manner. They were neither interested nor willing to hold off leaving the airport because one of their passengers was not on board when she should be. She did make it to the airport in time, checked her bag and then was sidetracked at an enticing gift shop. Before she knew it, time -her nemesis - got away from her.

Consequently, Jaime arrived at the gate some three minutes after take-off time and watched her plane taxi down the runway without her.

"Darn!" she exclaimed, stamping her foot. It was her own fault, and nobody knew that better than Jaime. But knowing that…and being angry at herself…didn't get her on that plane. It was the only flight of the day to Albany Airport, which had all sorts of dire consequences. First, she would miss her connection in Albany to her final destination. A limo was scheduled to pick her up at the airport and take her to the resort in the Catskills, but that was now a moot point. Second, her resort room reservation -- too late to cancel -- would charge her credit card for the night when she didn't show up. Third, she would miss her entire weekend away. No point in going for just one day.

To her credit, Jaime had tried various little tricks to fool herself into being on time. She set her watch and clock at home fifteen minutes ahead. She marked her appointment calendar for a one o'clock meeting when it was really scheduled for two. (But occasionally she missed it by an entire day!) Her friends knew enough to tell Jaime that the party was starting at least half an hour before it actually was. However, Jaime's mind was aware of all of these tricks and seemed to conspire to make her late anyway! In despair and frustration, she stamped her foot again and then sat down in one of the chairs at the gate, unsure of what to do next.

"Excuse me, miss," a tall, distinguished elderly gentlemen asked, "Did you miss your plane?"

"Yes, and it was the only one to Albany today, which means I won't be able to get to the resort in the Catskills for my weekend vacation. There's no point in going tomorrow afternoon and then coming back the next day," she replied, surprising herself by giving the stranger so much information. She looked at him closely. Did she know him? He seemed very familiar…

"We're you by any chance going to the Leeds?" he asked.

"Why, yes, I was. Have you been there?"

"Several times. In fact, that's where I am headed now. I have a private plane at my disposal and my limo is meeting me in Albany. I don't suppose you'd consider letting me give you a lift?"

Jaime knew it wasn't a good idea. How many times had her mother warned her about strangers and accepting rides when she was younger! This wasn't just a ride…this was taking off in a plane with a man she didn't know and trusting that he was telling the truth! No, it wasn't a good idea at all.

"You're very kind," she said and found herself continuing, "I'd be most grateful. This is my first weekend away in two years and I really don't want to miss a whole day of it."

"I'll have my chauffeur pick up your bag at the airport. My name is Martin Hayes, and you are…"

Martin Hayes! No wonder he looked familiar. Martin Hayes was very high profile and a well-known professor at the University. He had been on the news several times; something about a research project he was working on having to do with…what was it again…oh, yes, time travel!

"Jaime Cunningham, "she said hastily, realizing that she had been staring. "I really appreciate this, Professor Hayes."

"Not at all, Miss Cunningham, and please call me Martin. We will be spending three hours together on the plane and there is no need for formality."

"Then you should call me Jaime. I'm really fascinated with your project. I've been reading about it in the newspaper." Martin picked up her carry-on bag and they began walking down the concourse. A few minutes later, they went through a door and then they were walking along the runway to a hanger where a small plane sat. Jaime was very impressed that the security guard at the door had just smiled, nodded and touched his hat as they passed. Obviously Martin Hayes was well known at the airport also.

In a matter of minutes, they were seated in the small but luxurious plane. "We have provisions on board and we'll be served luncheon as soon as we are in the air. Am I correct that you didn't eat before you left, Jaime?"

'No, I didn't," she murmured, "I didn't have time…"

It was a most interesting trip. Lunch was gourmet…braised chicken breast with a delicate wine sauce and mushrooms, asparagus with Hollandaise sauce, tiny new potatoes in garlic butter, and delicious fresh rolls.

"This beats the snack pack I was expecting," Jaime sighed when the plates were removed.

Martin laughed. "I think we should wait for dessert, don't you? Would you like coffee or tea?"

"Tea, I think. I seldom drink coffee."

They moved to the lounge where they were served tea and continued their luncheon conversation about Martin's project.

"So exactly how does this work?" asked Jaime, curled comfortably on the lounge with her feet tucked under her.

"Well, I haven't quite gotten a handle on the technology, "said Martin with a slight frown. "I've managed to send objects through the machine to somewhere, but I'm not exactly sure they got to their destination. When you're dealing with the past, it's hard to track. They disappeared, but where they appeared is anybody's guess. I think I have the controls correct, and I don't try to send anything back too far… just a few days."

"Maybe you should try sending things forward," suggested Jaime. "If you sent…say, a ball…forward into tomorrow, then tomorrow you would be able to see if it was there."

"Makes sense. I've been focusing on going into the past with this machine. But I don't see why it wouldn't work just as well into the future."

"Is it big enough to send a person?"

"Yes, but that's very risky. I'm not ready to even attempt anything live yet. When I do, it won't be a person…probably a small animal."

Jaime pondered that for a minute. What if…what if this machine could somehow help her with her "time problem?"

"Just how sensitive are the controls? I mean, could you set them for only an hour or two rather than days?"

I could adjust them for any amount of time I choose, I suppose."

Martin liked her idea about using the future instead of the past, and they were deep in conversation about it when the pilot announced that they were landing. Both hastened to fasten their seat belts and the subject was dropped.

The plane taxied to the private hanger area, and the long blue limo was waiting. The chauffeur had, per Martin's phone call from the airport, collected Jaime's bag, as the plane she missed had landed some twenty minutes earlier.

It was a pleasant ride to the resort. Martin related some of his travel experiences over the years and the subject of the time machine was temporarily forgotten. He dropped her off at the front door to check in. From their conversation, Jaime realized that he had a more or less permanent status at the resort and came and went whenever he pleased. Martin suggested they meet for dinner the next evening and she quickly accepted.

Thanks to Martin, Jaime apparently made the deadline for check-in time because no one questioned her or her reservation, which she felt was one step up from her usual practice. Finally, she had a whole two days to do nothing, not expected to be anywhere at any particular time. She was in control, not at the mercy of Time! She gave herself over to a long luxurious soak in the sauna tub in her room, staying in the water until <u>she</u> wanted to leave. Then she dressed in a simple summer shift and sandals and left the room looking for someplace for dinner.

Wonder of wonders, dinner was still being served, and no one seemed in a big hurry to feed her and shove her out the door, as had happened in so many restaurants back home--due to her lack of time consciousness. She ate a small but leisurely dinner, and there were still patrons eating when she left. She took the opportunity to scout out the amenities, strolling by the huge pool, which extended under a wall and into a building; the gardens with paved paths lined with fragrant flowers and interesting Greek-type statues scattered here and there; and even the many shops which were still open despite it being very late.

With a start, Jaime realized that she had not seen a clock since she checked in. Even the lobby didn't have a time piece on display. And she had no idea what time it actually was. Did it matter? Not a bit! She laughed out loud as she realized she had finally found a place where she fit. Apparently time didn't matter to anyone here either!

Jaime slept soundly and awoke late, which was a surprise since she usually didn't rest well in a strange bed. Again she was aware there was no clock in the room, and the battery in her watch had apparently died. Thankfully, she shed the watch, tucking it in the corner of her suitcase. She never liked wearing one anyway, and now she had a perfect excuse not to. Hastily she grabbed her clam diggers and a shell top and left her room looking for food.

"Am I too late for breakfast?" she asked as she arrived at the restaurant a little out of breath.

"Of course not. Please come in and we'll have your breakfast ready in a few minutes." And they did. Golden waffles, scrambled eggs, bacon crisp and tasty. Jaime felt a little guilty eating so much, and knew her waistline would suffer from it, but it was so good she didn't care.

She decided to try the unique indoor/outdoor pool and went back to her room for her swimsuit. The water was delightful, exactly the temperature she liked. She was able to swim outside, then duck under the wall and swim inside, where she found both a hot tub and a sauna. No one to pressure her, no schedule to keep, she stayed and enjoyed herself for as long as she liked.

After she left the pool and was dressed again, she strolled down the winding paths through the gardens in the afternoon sunlight. Jaime wandered along until she reached a large pond. Huge goldfish swam through the rippled shadows. Mesmerized, Jaime sat and watched as they moved lazily around the pond, stopping occasionally to nibble at a plant. She had no idea how long she sat there, but the sun was moving lower in the sky and she remembered her dinner engagement. She strolled back to her room to shower and change before realizing she had no idea what time she was supposed to meet Martin…and had no way of knowing what time it was then even if she had.

Taking a chance, she scooped up her evening bag and headed for the restaurant, noting that the door was closed and locked and a large arrow pointed down the hall. Shrugging her shoulders, she followed the arrows through a set of double doors and found herself in a restaurant... not the same one as she had eaten in the previous evening, but even more opulent. The curtains were shimmering gold velvet; the tables had gleaming glass tops and chairs padded with white satin. As she entered, she was immediately escorted to a corner table as Martin stood at her arrival.

"Oh, dear, were you waiting long?" she asked, and he smiled and shook his head.

"Just arrived. No, you aren't late. You won't have to worry about being late here...there's no such thing." He added with a chuckle.

Within minutes, drinks were served, the waiter took their order and Martin leaned back in his chair.

"Now," he said, "I have a proposition for you. I know you have only the weekend here, but I thought you might like to spend some off it giving me a hand with my time machine."

"Really? Oh, Martin, I would like nothing better!" Jaime exclaimed. "I always felt somehow time controlled me...I would love the chance to help you control it! Do you have it here?"

"This is where I do work. Nowhere else would be appropriate."

Jaime thought that was a strange thing to say, but she was too excited to question him about it. "When can we do this?"

"I'll send the limo for you tomorrow morning, and then Carl can see that you get back to the airport for your flight home," Martin said, and then changed the subject as their dinner arrived.

Before they parted, Jaime asked, "What time should I be ready?"

"Don't worry. Carl will be there when you are."

That was also a strange thing to say, thought Jaime, but since time didn't seem to matter here, what difference did it make? She would just get up and get ready tomorrow morning and expect the car would be there when it got there.

As she exited the elevator the next morning, she saw the limo just pulling up outside. Perfect timing, she thought, and then shuddered. There was no such thing. Time was not her friend...it had always been her enemy. Strange as it may seem, it rather bothered her that she was never late...apparently <u>couldn't</u> be late...here.

Busy watching the beautiful scenery they passed, Jaime had no idea how long it was before the limo pulled up to Martin's cabin…well, it really wasn't a cabin, it was more like a house…a very large house. Jaime was in awe. Martin met her at the door and escorted her to the patio where a delightful breakfast of fresh fruit and cinnamon rolls awaited.

When they finished eating, Martin took her to a large room in back of the house full of electronics, computers and fascinating pieces of equipment. In the corner was what Martin pointed out as the Time Machine. It didn't look very imposing at all. Rather like a large wooden box with a seat in front of a small computer, and a set of controls which reminded Jaime of the controls on a computer game. If she had not read the newspaper articles on this research, she would be tempted to think it was some kind of joke.

Martin was very serious, however. They started by reviewing some of the records of his experiments. It was fascinating as she had never been exposed to any kind of scientific experiments before. Everything was documented in painstaking detail. Explanation of how the concept worked, and why, was a document of some fifty pages, and Jaime read it all, even though some of the technical and scientific words were totally unfamiliar. She was even more confused when she finished, because she thought she had a relatively good grasp of the concept before reading the manual.

"Martin, am I to understand, and maybe I am far off the mark, that you are saying there is <u>no such thing as Time</u>?"

"Exactly. Time is a concept of man. In reality, Time is a continuum, Jaime. There is no beginning and no end. There is no past and no future…just the <u>now</u>. We only are aware of "time" because we are in a specific place in the "time line." Look at it this way. Suppose you were on a train riding across the countryside. You see a tree up ahead out the window. That is in your future. Within a certain period of 'time' the tree shows up outside window where you are sitting, in your present. But as the train continues--as our concept of time continues--the tree is then behind you, or in your past.

"If you were up in an airplane over the train," he continued, "You would see the tree all the time…you would see the past, present and the future all at once."

It made a lot of sense…at least, what she could actually grasp of it.

"So really, there is no such thing as 'time' except what man has designated?" she queried.

"Exactly. Man made the clocks and watches, man set schedules. The only natural 'passing of time' is the rising and setting of the sun, and if we were not on earth, that wouldn't even be relevant."

"So there is no reason why, given the right equipment, we can't go back into the 'past' or even into the 'future?'" ventured Jaime.

"That's the concept. Now all we have to do is make the equipment work," said Martin. "Shall we try your future theory?"

Martin carefully manipulated the computer and the controls inside the box. "We'll start with an hour, shall we? I've set the coordinates so the ball should appear in this room somewhere." He put a baseball marked with an X on the seat, shut the door and pushed the buttons on the panel. There was an odd whirring noise, the lights blinked in the room, and when he opened the box, the ball was gone.

"Now," he declared, "My stomach tells me that it would like some lunch. How about yours?"

Jaime was suddenly aware that she was very hungry. She had been so fascinated with their activities that it didn't even register. They adjourned to the patio, where a fresh salad, with iced tea, tiny turkey sandwiches and a delicious potato salad was already laid out on the table. How does he do that? she wondered. He had made no phone calls nor contacted anyone outside the room where they had been working, but there was lunch…just as if it had been ordered.

They lingered over iced tea until Martin, as if he had received some kind of psychic signal, stood and said, "Let's see what our experiment 'hath wrought'."

As he opened the door to the lab, Jaime saw the ball sitting in the middle of the floor. "It worked!" she cried, jubilantly. "We sent the ball into the future!"

"So it did," replied Martin mildly. "But the ball is a physical object.

I wonder how it would work with --a living thing. What should we plan to do next, do you think?"

"I think you should send me. "

Martin shook his head emphatically. "It's too soon to try humans," he said. "I don't know how safe it is."

"Martin, look. If your theory is right...like with the train ride you just told me about, it should be perfectly safe. You said yourself that time is man's invention."

"I can't be responsible if something should happen to you. What if you couldn't get back..."

"I'm not planning to 'get back.' Listen, I've always had this thing with Time. I can't seem to ever get to where I'm going when I'm supposed to. I have a theory also. If you send me into the future...say, just half an hour...maybe, just maybe, I'll be where I'm supposed to be. I think I am constantly operating in the past...not far in the past, but just like half an hour or so. All you would be doing is moving my body to catch up to where it should be. Man may have been responsible for counting time, but you have no idea how stressful and frustrating it is to never, never, <u>never</u> be able to get to where you are supposed to be when you are supposed to be there!"

Martin sat thinking as Jaime shifted in her chair. She knew this would work. Perhaps this was even why she was here and why she missed her plane. He had to agree...he simply had to agree!

"I may regret this, but you do make sense. The machine may not even work with humans or any living thing. But I guess I'm willing to try if you are."

Jaime was willing and in fact eager. She waited impatiently while Martin set the controls and then checked and double checked them. She was going into the future just thirty minutes, and he didn't want any screw-ups or mistakes to send her back into the past or too far ahead. As long as it was only half an hour, he could handle that.

At last he opened the door and motioned Jaime inside. She sat gingerly on the seat and squeezed her eyes shut as Martin closed the door to the box.

Instantly she opened her eyes to find herself on a chair in the middle of the room.

"It worked, dear girl!" exclaimed Martin gleefully. "You were gone for half an hour and just appeared on the chair out of nowhere. How do you feel?"

Gingerly she stood up, moved her arms and legs. "Fine, I think. I'm all in one piece. I do feel a little different, but I can't explain it."

"And what happened while you were gone for that half hour?" he asked.

"No idea. I was not even aware that I was anywhere. One second I was in the box and the next second I was on the chair out in the room. I don't know that anything changed, but it was definitely an experience. Martin, thank you so much for letting me work with you and listening to my crazy theory. This has been the best day I've ever spent!"

"No, Jaime, thanks to you, I've made great strides in my work. You've been more help than you know. Now Carl should be here shortly to take you back to Albany to catch your plane home. Here's my card. Please let me know if you have any side effects from your little journey into the future."

A tap on the door announced that Carl was, indeed, there. Again, she wondered briefly how Martin knew what time it was when there were no clocks or watches around.

Carl took her back to her room, where she packed quickly and then checked out. Then she was on her way to the airport. She arrived an hour before flight time, read a magazine while sitting at the gate, and boarded the plane on time. During the flight home, she spent a lot of time musing over the events of the past weekend. The more she thought about it, the more she wondered how the place functioned without any visible clocks. It was an odd way to run a resort, to say the least, but apparently very successful. Her day with Martin was even more interesting and the subject of most of her thoughts.

Monday morning Jaime arrived at work just before nine o'clock, shocking her boss and fellow workers. She left for lunch precisely at noon and was back before one. The entire week seemed strange, because she was never late, never racing the clock for anything. Her sister called to invite her to dinner on Wednesday, telling her to be sure and be there before five thirty.

"Sally, dear, you know you never eat before six. I'll be there at ten of six." And she was.

By Friday she knew the trip into the future had worked as she planned. She didn't feel stressed, her watch suddenly came back to life and was working fine, and she set it for the correct time, not fifteen minutes fast. She never missed a deadline, never arrived after the store or bank had closed, never "lost track of time" as had been her habit to do frequently in the past.

Saturday morning, she called Martin.

"Just wanted you to know how well our little experiment worked," she said. "I've had absolutely no side effects, except that I don't have a time problem anymore. I no longer feel as if time controls me. And best of all, I no longer have the stress of trying to deal with it."

"Wonderful, Jaime. That's good news. I have a very big and important experiment planned for this afternoon, and if it goes well, you'll be hearing about it."

On Monday morning, Jaime picked up the newspaper that was delivered to her apartment. Open mouthed, she stared at the headlines:

"Time Travel Researcher Disappears."

The article went on to say that Martin had left a message that he was using himself as a guinea pig in his time machine and was propelling himself forward into the future. Of course, no one believed in time travel and there was a huge investigation into the possibility of foul play. However, they could find no clues, no evidence, nothing out of the ordinary in his lab. The police noticed that the time machine was set for a date three years in the future.

Jaime put down the paper and smiled. And when her mail arrived that afternoon, she smiled even wider. The letter read:

"By now you've heard about my experiment. You can no longer claim to be the only person who has traveled through time, my dear. This is what my entire life and all my research has been geared toward. Would you meet me in your future for dinner? I'll have a great deal of information to share with you. I'll be at Leeds in the restaurant on the 23rd of June, three years from now. As you already know, time doesn't matter at Leeds. Whenever you arrive, I will be waiting. I may even let you talk me into sending you on another trip in the machine. Regards, Martin"

Whisperings

The noise was loud enough to wake the dead. Who it woke, however, was Sarah. She opened her eyes, being unaware for the moment of what had disturbed her. She was warm and comfortable. It was dark outside. The clock on the nightstand read 2:05 a.m. All was calm and quiet.

Then she saw it - just a flicker reflected on her windowpane. She hesitated for a moment, but a second flicker drew her out of bed and over to the window. The building across the street was on fire. Seconds after she reached the window, an explosion turned it into a blazing inferno. Before she could reach for the phone by her bed, she heard sirens. Three fire trucks and two police cars came screaming around the corner. She continued to watch for several minutes but realized that there was a real possibility that her building could be in danger.

Hurriedly she dressed in jeans and sweatshirt, grabbed her jacket and purse and went back to the window to watch the flurry of activity two stories below. Reluctant to leave her apartment if she didn't have to, Sarah pulled a chair up to the window so she could sit and wait to see what was going to happen.

After some two hours, it was obvious that they had things under control and the danger of the fire spreading was practically nil. As she pushed the chair back from the window, there was a loud knock on her door. Who could be knocking on her door at this hour?

"Who's there? What do you want?" This was not a neighborhood where she was willing to open the door to a stranger.

"Police. Open up."

Reluctantly she opened the door. Two men in uniform stood there, and she let them come in.

"Ma'am, we're looking for the arsonist that torched the building across the street," said one policeman bluntly. "Your window overlooks the building. Did you see anything just before the fire broke out?"

"I was asleep and I think an explosion woke me up. It was burning by the time I saw it...just before the second explosion."

The man looked at her a little suspiciously. "Asleep? You're fully dressed."

"I thought this place might be in danger, so I got dressed ready to go if I had *to.*"

"That makes sense," volunteered the other cop.

"Why would anyone want to burn that old warehouse?" Sarah asked. "It's been empty for as long as I can remember."

"That's what we're trying to find out, ma'am." He handed her a card. "Call this number if you see anything suspicious over there."

Sarah took the card, but thought it was a rather strange thing for a policeman to do. Why not just say to call the police? And what did they think was going to be going on after the building was already burned?

After they left, Sarah flopped down on the bed, reluctant to change back into her night clothes. She only had another hour she could sleep anyway. The events of the night ran through her mind. Had she seen anyone across the street? No, she was sure she hadn't. Who would torch an old empty building anyway? Why did the policemen act so strangely? And whose number was on the card they handed her. She had looked at it before lying down. There was only a number... no name... no address. Just a phone number. As an amateur mystery writer, she thought she might be able to gain some ideas from this situation for her next story.

Sarah dozed off and woke half an hour late, so she had no time to make coffee or grab breakfast. She threw on her coat, grabbed her purse, and ran down the stairs to her car parked in back of the building. As she pulled out of the driveway onto the street, she noticed a man attempting to pry open a door to the burned building across the street. The building was still smoldering a bit, and there were police tapes all around, but that didn't seem to faze the man.

Probably from the police department, she thought, but when she reached the next corner and stopped at the light, she poked around her purse for the phone number on the card. Should she call it? Deciding not to take a chance, she dialed the number from her cell phone.

"Yes?" It was a brusque voice at the other end.

"I was given this number by the police last night at the warehouse fire."

"So?'

"So do you want to know what's going on over there or not?"

"Yes."

"There's a man trying to get inside the building. He's inside the police tapes and he's prying open a door. Is he one of yours?"

"Thanks." The line was disconnected.

So much for being a good public citizen, she thought. Well, she did her duty. But that's the last time she would call <u>that</u> number. What a rude person! She worked late and was careful not to even look at the burned warehouse when she returned home. She had a salad for dinner, cleaned up the kitchen area, showered and headed for an early night in bed. Turning the TV channel to the news, she settled down for what she hoped would be an uneventful night. Surprisingly, there was only a passing mention about the fire, and she took that to mean it must not be any big deal. The media usually ferrets out and reports secrets, even when they shouldn't. After all, it was only an old empty warehouse and probably should have been torn down a long time ago, anyway.

Once again at 2:05 a.m. she woke suddenly for no apparent reason. It was quiet and dark. She had no idea what had caused her to suddenly wake up. Reluctantly she slid out of bed and padded to the kitchen for a drink of water. She had just dropped an ice cube in her glass when she heard a whisper. "Stop them."

She whirled around. She had turned on the light on the nightstand in her tiny studio apartment and she could see that there was no one there. A few seconds later the whisper came again, "Stop them."

Sarah started to panic. She was not normally a superstitious person, nor was she prone to imagination. Without thinking about it, she moved to the window and peeked through the drapes.

Something was going on across the street! Quickly she turned off the light and peered through the space between the curtains. Two men with flashlights were moving around near the building. Apparently they were looking for something. Well, they could just keep on looking. She had no intention of calling that rude man again, especially not at two in the morning! This was none of her business anyway, she thought, as she dialed the number.

"Yes."

"There are two men with flashlights looking for something in the burned-out warehouse." Without waiting for a reply, she hung up the phone. Then she returned to her spot at the window to see what would happen.

About five minutes later, she saw a black car with no headlights cruise slowly down the street, stopping before it reached the warehouse site. Two men slipped from the car, not even bothering to close the car doors. They moved close to the other buildings until they reached the warehouse. It was over in a few minutes. The two men with the flashlights spotted their attackers and fled. The two would-be captors jumped in the front seat of their car and sped off.

Well, that was that! She hoped she did the right thing. Then her mystery writer brain kicked in. What if... the policemen who came to her door really weren't... what if... the police were really the ones looking for something in the building and she alerted the criminals... what if...No, that didn't make sense, but then neither did the phone number she was calling. Well, it was over now. She'd just go back to bed and forget about it.

What she couldn't forget, however, was the whisper that she heard twice...and which may have been what woke her up in the first place. Reluctantly she returned to bed, but this time she turned on the nightstand light and left it on the rest of the night. Not that she was superstitious or believed in ghosts or anything. She just preferred to have the light on when she slept this time.

The next day was Saturday and Sarah was up earlier than usual. She made coffee and toast slathered with honey. Then she cleaned her studio apartment in less than an hour and spent another hour jotting down notes for a new mystery story she was writing. Finally, she tucked her cell phone in her pocket and threw her laundry in the basket to take to the laundromat down the street. All the time she kept the drapes closed tightly and made no effort to look out the window.

Maybe she should have! When she opened her door, laundry basket on her hip, she almost ran into two very large men standing outside her apartment. One of them pushed her back inside as they came in and closed the door behind them.

'Who are you? What do you want?" Sarah asked, her voice quavering.

One man went to the window and roughly pulled the drapes back. "You're right, Joe. This is the perfect spot. We got a great view from here."

Joe shoved Sarah into a chair and tossed her purse and laundry basket on the floor.

"You ain't goin' nowhere, honey. We need your apartment for awhile."

The thug at the window turned and ordered gruffly, "Tie her up, Bud," and turned back to the window.

"Wait, you don't have to tie me up. I'm not going to move off this chair."

"You sure ain't, honey," Bud agreed, and proceeded to pull a roll of twine from his pocket, tie her hands together and wind the twine around the chair several times. Sarah knew yelling was worthless. The building was being renovated and she was, at the moment, the only tenant. The work crew wasn't there on weekends. All screaming would do was make them mad, and Lord knows what they were capable of. She bit her lip and kept her mouth shut.

For the next hour, all they did was stand and look out the window. Apparently nothing was happening across the street of any interest to them and she hoped they would get tired of it and just leave. Unfortunately, she could identify them, and that was not a good thing at this point.

"'Wait. Who's that?" Bud asked, staring out the window. Joe turned and peered out between the drapes.

"Nobody. Just an old jakey bum. Look at'em stagger. Gotta be drunk as a skunk even this early in the mornin'. Probably homeless and thinks he found a place to crash."

"Want I should go over there and discourage 'im?"

"Naw. Not worth showing yerself. Let 'im be. He ain't no threat. We'll be okay, as long as the cops don't go diggin' today. Should be able to find it and move out after it gets dark."

"Joe, can't we let the broad off the chair? I really need a cup of java and she could make it for us."

"Maybe she could make us some chow, too," came the snide remark, but Sarah ignored the tone of voice.

"Sure, I make a great cup of coffee. And I'm not a bad cook either. You know I can't go anywhere, and I'm sure you know there's nobody else in the building, so please just untie me." Sarah's wrists were getting sore from the twine rubbing and she was really very thirsty.

"Aw, go ahead. Let'er loose. She's only a little thing. If she tries to get away, I'm sure one of us can stop her real easy." So, Sarah was untied, and got permission to use kitchen area after Bud checked it to see that there no weapons of mass destruction there. He gave his partner the two small steak knives from the drawer that were the only sharp knives she owned.

She made a pot of coffee, noticing that her hands shook only a little, and was proud of herself for remaining so calm. There was still the problem of identifying the two thugs and she hoped they wouldn't feel compelled to shoot her before they left. Still no activity out the window. The homeless man had apparently found his way inside the building, what was left of it, and was probably curled up in a corner somewhere, sleeping it off.

Sarah was ordered to make sandwiches, and then was allowed to sit in the chair and read, which she pretended to do although concentration on a book was impossible. Around six in the evening, as it was getting dark, she heard a whisper in her ear. "Lock yourself in the bathroom." She quickly looked around, but the two thugs were glued to the window and talking quietly between themselves. Again the whisper just behind her head, "Lock yourself in the bathroom...now."

Not one to miss an opportunity, and she certainly wasn't going to question the chance, Sarah asked, "Gentlemen, is it all right if I go to the bathroom?"

"Bud, check the john out and make sure there's nuttin' dangerous in there." Bud did at he was told and apparently it passed inspection.

"Sure, go ahead," replied Joe, only glancing her way. Apparently they realized she was no threat to them. Quickly Sarah went inside the bathroom and locked the door. She was thankful that she had her cell phone in her pants pocket and they hadn't found it. She pulled it out and punched send, and it automatically rang the last number she had called...the rude man.

As soon as the phone stopped ringing, she whispered," They're in my apartment. Help," and then hung up, hoping there was someone on the other end and not a machine. Not knowing what else to do, she curled up inside the tub, thinking at least it would be some protection if they started shooting through the door.

Minutes later there was a loud crash, sounds of a scuffle, and someone yelled, "Drop the gun and put your hands behind your head." Shortly after, there was a knock on the bathroom door.

"You can come out now. It's okay," and she quickly unlocked the door. Her apartment was somewhat of a shambles. Apparently Joe and Bud didn't take kindly to being wrestled to the floor, but they were subdued, handcuffed and being dragged out the door by several policemen. To her surprise, the man who told her to come out was dressed in rags, had a scraggly beard and an old felt hat. It dawned on her that this was the "jakey bum" that Joe had seen out the window.

Shaken, Sarah sat on the chair and watched the policemen efficiently escort their prisoners out the door, then return the overturned chairs and table to their rightful spots. They assured her that someone would come within the hour and fix the door they had broken down. When everyone had left and the man dressed in rags was about to leave, Sarah stopped him.

Please, I think I deserve an explanation. What exactly is going on?"

The tale would certainly give her enough ideas for her next mystery story. It seemed that the warehouse was owned by an elderly man who had recently passed away. He was a well known and respected city official, but his two sons were on the shady side of the law. Unbeknownst to their father, they were using the warehouse to store stolen property. They had a ledger in the warehouse but were unable to retrieve it before the fire. The fire itself was very suspicious, since there was no indication that it had been set deliberately, and there was no electricity or fuel inside to account for its mysterious origin.

Because everyone loved Old Man Edgar, they were trying to protect his good name but still not be lenient with his sons. Dan, the undercover cop whose number Sarah had been given, had portrayed himself as a homeless bum to avoid alerting the two thugs while he searched. He found the ledger undamaged, hidden inside an old filing cabinet. It recorded all the names, dates and destinations of the stolen property, which was quite an enormous sum and involved a great many people. The records actually would break up a large criminal ring of thieves.

Sarah's phone message had reached him, but he had already had his own whispered message ten minutes before, telling him to go to her apartment through the back as the front was being watched and alerting him that she would be hiding in the bathroom. The police were already in the building and on their way upstairs when she called.

Sarah wasn't going to mention the whispered messages she had been receiving, but found herself telling Dan, since he shared her experience and wouldn't think she was crazy.

"What do you think it was?" she asked, a little fearfully. "Is this place haunted?"

"I don't want to freak you out, but I have to tell you...the voice I heard? It was the old man's. He had throat cancer and could only speak in a whisper. I swear to God that was his voice."

"I'm not sure I believe in ghosts, but those whispers warned me that someone was poking around at 2 a.m. when I called you, and the same voice told me to lock myself in the bathroom just before you came. I can't pretend it didn't happen."

"Old Man Edgar loved those boys, but they were bad clear through. As long as he was alive, he kept them in line, but after he got sick and then died, they just headed down the wrong path full speed. I wouldn't be surprised if the old man set the place on fire himself to flush them out."

"But he's been dead for ... Oh, well, I guess if he can make us hear him, he can do other things. It certainly isn't impossible..."

"Are you afraid to stay here alone now?" Dan asked.

"Good heavens, no. Those whispers never hurt me ... in fact they saved me, so I can't imagine the old gentleman doing anything bad. In fact, it's sorta comforting knowing he's watching out for me."

"Then I'll be going. Thanks so much for your help. And we would appreciate it if you could keep this little episode to yourself. We do want to protect Old Man Edgar's good name if we can."

"Ask her out to dinner, dunce," came a loud raspy whisper. Both Dan and Sarah, startled, looked around the room and then at each other.

"Well, I suppose we better do as we're told," laughed Dan. "You did hear what I heard, right?"

"Loud and clear," replied Sarah with a smile.

"Then we'll have to stop by my apartment so I can change. I don't think you want a jakey bum taking you to dinner."

"Hold the fort, Mr. Edgar," she called out as she grabbed her purse and coat.

And they both swore they heard a whispery chuckle before they shut the door.

A Hawley House Weekend

"I'd rather you went without me," Miranda said quietly. "I really am not interested in that sort of thing."

"Nonsense. Where's your sense of adventure?" asked her sister, Kate, tossing her long blonde curls the way she always did when annoyed. Kate always felt that at seventeen…almost eighteen…she should be allowed to do more things than she was. Her mother was like the proverbial "clinging vine," and put more restrictions than necessary on her activities. This trip would be good for both of them, since Miranda was basically as homebound as she was.

"Just the same, this isn't my idea of an adventure…more like a waste of time."

Kate snorted. "Admit it, Miranda. You're just scared."

"I'm just practical. You and I both know, Kate, there are no such things as ghosts." Miranda stood up to leave the room, effectively terminating the conversation and the subject.

Kate grabbed her arm. "Please, Miranda. Don't ruin this for me. If you don't go, you know Mom won't let me go and it's only for a weekend. Don't be a spoil sport!"

"Whining doesn't become you, Katherine Jane. Why is this so important to you?"

"Even Robbie's big brother is going so he can go. It's not like we'll be alone there. There's a whole group of people going, and I just think it'll be lots of fun."

"And the main reason is that Robbie will be there, right? Well, if it's that important to you, I suppose I could postpone my weekend plans and go with you." Miranda relented reluctantly with a sigh. Postponing her plans wasn't much of a hardship…it involved laundry, gardening and cleaning the storeroom in the basement. Even so, there was probably nothing she wanted to do less than spend a weekend with a group of young adults in a haunted house.

Lord knows their mother kept a tight rein on Kate, who would be eighteen in less than three weeks. She wasn't even allowed to date except in a group, and Kate unfortunately believed that her sister was in full accord with their mother. But although Miranda really was not in agreement, her mother made it clear that she had no say in the matter. Miranda felt that keeping too much control on a girl Kate's age would only lead to rebellion and worse; her mother seemed to be afraid that the teenager would get herself in trouble if she was allowed any freedom at all.

A weekend in a haunted house would get them both away from that restriction and who knows…it might be fun after all. Couldn't be much worse than a scary movie, and Kate loved those, so at least she would have fun. Miranda loved her younger sister and it wasn't that much of a sacrifice to be bored for a couple of days so Kate could enjoy herself.

Even with Miranda agreeing to go, it was a struggle to get their mother to agree, but she finally did very reluctantly. They left on a Saturday morning with the group on a chartered bus. There were eight teenagers ranging from seventeen to nineteen, and four chaperones--Miranda being one of them. She was probably more mature for her age than most twenty-five-year-olds, and the other chaperones were a bit older. Robbie's brother Greg, according to Kate, was in his late twenties and the two others, one male and one female, were probably thirty or more.

Miranda sat in the back with the other woman, who introduced herself as Allison. She was on the trip simply because she loved stories about ghosts and thought it would be a chance to actually see one. Her brother Ralph was the other chaperone and didn't have an opinion one way or another. He thought it was a little silly but was indulging his sister.

Kate was sitting up front, presumably next to Robbie, and from the laughter and giggling, it was obvious she was having a great time. Miranda smiled and was glad she came. Kate had little enough pleasure in her life and she was really a very good kid.

Unbeknownst to Kate, Miranda was pressuring their mother to allow her sister to go to a college away from home rather than the local university. So far she hadn't succeeded, but persistence was one of her good points and she believed sooner or later Mother would relent. Miranda hadn't been allowed to go away to college, and now she felt trapped at home with a widowed and very dependent parent who pleaded illness when things weren't going her way and who controlled her entire household with an iron fist. Miranda wanted her sister to escape that whole scenario, if possible.

Allison chattered most of the way, which didn't require much input from Miranda, leaving her free to observe the rest of the passengers. Robbie's brother Greg…now there was a good-looking man! She imagined he must be sacrificing his social life to accompany his brother on this trip. Allison's brother Ralph, on the other hand, seemed rather withdrawn and had his nose in a book most of the trip.

Their destination was a good half hour ride from the nearest point of civilization. The driveway was long, narrow and lined with scraggly trees. The house hadn't seen a coat of paint for at least thirty years and the only color around was a field of dandelions which served as a front yard. All in all, whoever created it did a marvelous job making it look deserted and …well, haunted.

The bus dropped them off and then left, effectively stranding the group until it returned on Sunday evening…at least, Miranda hoped it would be back then. Reminding herself that it was all contrived and someone had done a great job with atmosphere, she picked up her overnight bag and followed the group who trudged up the stairs onto the porch. The door was open, and they all trooped inside. Whoever expected them was apparently not around...all was quiet and no one could locate a light switch.

Inside the large living room was a table on which stood a number of candles in holders and a box of matches. No electric lights, Miranda guessed. Marvelous! She had planned to spend her evenings reading in her room...guess that was out.

"Do you think we weren't expected?" said a voice in her ear. Startled, she spun around and almost collided with Robbie's brother.

"Oh, I'm sure we were. They were quick to take our money so I can't imagine we weren't. This is probably just part of the atmosphere to get us in the mood before the 'ghosts' show up."

"I take it you're a skeptic?" Greg asked with raised eyebrows.

"Of course. Aren't you?"

"Not exactly. I'm willing to have an open mind. If there are such things as ghosts, we should be convinced by the end of this weekend."

Just then Kate came over dragging a shy young man by the arm.

"Miranda, this is Robbie, and I see you've already met his brother. Robbie, my sister Miranda."

Robbie blushed and shook Miranda's hand. Amused, Miranda solemnly acknowledged the introduction. Kate would have this young man under her thumb in no time.

They all turned as a middle-aged lady, huffing and puffing, came clattering down the stairs, wiping her hands on her apron.

"I'm so sorry...I'm Mrs. Beale. You're a bit early and I was just finishing up making the beds. Welcome to Hawley House."

The room suddenly turned darker. "Oh, dear, we're expecting a rainstorm today. I'm so glad you arrived and got inside before it broke. Sometimes we have a lot of lightning and thunder with it, and it always seems to rain pretty hard."

Seconds later, a peal of thunder shook the house, causing some of the girls to scream and grab the nearest person.

"Wonder how they managed that," murmured Miranda.

"Couldn't," grinned Greg, "We're just lucky, I guess. That's all that was missing for a full-fledged haunting."

"I'll show you to your rooms and then fix us a nice luncheon."

Mrs. Beale seemed to take the weather and the group in stride. They followed her up the stairs to the second floor where she assigned the rooms. Kate was in the same room with Miranda, much to her relief. Ralph and Greg were each sharing a room with another young man, and the other guests were paired up two to a room.

Contrary to what they had first believed, there was electricity and electric lights, although they didn't seem to be very effective. Apparently one of the owners who planned to renovate the house had them installed. The ceiling lights were way too high to throw much light, and there seemed to be only one or two plugs per room. The fireplaces were lit both up and downstairs to take the chill off the rooms.

Their bedroom was large and dim. Rain beat against the windows and Miranda thought she had never seen such ominous black clouds. They left their bags on the beds and went back downstairs.

Mrs. Beale had a tasty lunch prepared of fried chicken, potato salad, a green salad, and iced tea. They ate in the dining room and watched the rain streaming down the tall windows, interspersed with flashes of lightning and claps of thunder. While they ate, Mrs. Beale told them a little of the history of Hawley House.

It seems that in the mid-twentieth century, there were three deaths in the house, all within a six-month period. All were assumed to be murders, although no one was ever charged and the ghosts of the victims reportedly cannot rest until the murderer is identified and caught.

"At this late date, that'll never happen," murmured Miranda to Greg, who was seated next to her.

According to Mrs. Beale, Hawley House was unoccupied for two decades because of the strange lights and noises. Then each time someone purchased the property with the intention of either renovating it or tearing it down, they met with an untimely death or accident. The electricity, she said, was installed by one of the owners before he met his early demise. The present owner never visited the house or attempted any changes. The taxes were paid every year, but no one ever came forward to make any claim on the property. The lawyers who forward the tax money were charged with hiring Mrs. Beale and collected the funds from the excursions held six times a year, such as the one they were presently on. The funds, according to Mrs. Beale, barely cover the taxes and her salary, and the owner wished to remain anonymous and have no other connection with Hawley House.

"Strangely enough," concluded Mrs. Beale, "we always seem to have a thunderstorm when we have guests. Please feel free to explore the house at your leisure. You are not allowed to explore the basement or the attic, however, and you would be well advised to move about in groups of at least two or three. Later this evening after dinner, we will have a séance in the library for anyone who wishes to attend. Sometimes nothing at all happens, and sometimes we have a great deal of activity. There are no guarantees, but you are welcome to be present."

"Wouldn't miss it for the world," said Greg softly to Miranda.

"Well, I would. Just not interested in parlor tricks."

"Afraid something will change your mind? Cum'on, that seems to be the only entertainment planned for this weekend. I'm sure your sister will want to attend."

"We'll see," she replied noncommittally.

The guests went off in groups exploring the house, which consisted of three floors. Some of the braver boys decided to check out the attic but found the door locked, as was the basement door. One bragged that he would be willing to crawl through the basement window, except that it was raining too hard to go outside.

An old-fashioned pump organ in the music room was put to use as Allison, surprising everyone, knew how to play it. Even with the music and the fireplaces, the house had a rather ominous aura. Miranda was disturbed because she believed she was too practical to be affected by some vague promise of ghosts and hauntings; yet she couldn't ignore the way the house made her feel…jumpy, nervous and uncomfortable, like someone was always watching her. She considered going into the library, finding a book and reading, but the idea of being in there alone didn't appeal to her. Unable to come up with a better reason for her jumpiness, she blamed it on the weather and stayed with some of the group in the music room.

By dinnertime, the weather had not changed. Everyone gathered in the dining room for a hearty homemade stew, hot bread and salad. The explorers had found nothing of any interest on either the third floor or the second, except for several old paintings of people that, Kate said, looked like they had been eating lemons. No one reported running across anything suspicious or "ghost-like," and they all professed to be interested in the séance, or as Greg put it, the evening's entertainment.

Miranda still was reluctant to attend, but no one else declined and between Kate and Greg's urgings, she agreed to participate...or at least sit in to see what went on. Perhaps she, being a disbelieving observer, could figure out what the trick was, if a ghost "appeared."

A clap of thunder, louder than any before, followed a brilliant flash of lightning and the electricity went out...not that it was much light to begin with, but it left the room dark instead of dim, and the candle flames danced and cast shadows on the wall. The girls moved closer to the guys and grabbed their hands or arms. Miranda resisted the impulse to grab Greg's hand. She knew no one could control the weather, but it certainly was convenient if, as Mrs. Beale said, it always stormed when they had guests which apparently was every other month. Her mind wandered a bit and she wondered what Mrs. Beale did the rest of the year.

The object of her wondering gathered the group into the library and seated them around the large oak table. She sat with her back toward the sliding glass doors and lit three large white candles on the table. The group huddled on the chairs a bit fearfully.

Mrs. Beale began to intone some sort of chant and suddenly the wind outside died down and the rain slowed to a sprinkle and then stopped altogether. Then, despite the fact that there was no breeze in the room, the candle flames began to flicker.

"Have we made contact?" asked Mrs. Beale in a rather eerie voice.

"You have," came a soft voice out of the darkness from the corner of the room. Several girls shrieked and the boys gasped.

Of course...she has a helper hidden here, thought Miranda. This might prove to be entertaining after all.

"I was known as Robert Bennett," said the disembodied voice. "I am one of the victims of Hawley House."

"We have not made contact with you before," said Mrs. Beale. "What have you come to tell us?"

"I come with a warning. It is not safe here. He who took our lives is now on the other side and seeks to destroy."

"Why? These people have done nothing to him."

"He is angry because he is no longer in your world. For all of the victims to which he brought death, he missed the one he wished to destroy, and now it is too late."

"So what will happen now?" asked Mrs. Beale, her voice shaking.

"He will destroy the house and all who are within," intoned the spirit being.

With that, Kate leaped to her feet, screamed and ran out the door. Robbie ran after her, closely followed by Miranda and Greg. They caught up to the two halfway up the stairs and stopped them. "Kate, stop. You have to know it's a trick…just a parlor trick. I'm sure there was another person hiding in the room acting as the spirit…" Miranda began.

Greg interrupted grimly, "Whether it's true or not, we aren't going to stay here and take a chance. He said the house would be destroyed… well, I don't intend to be inside if it is." He produced a cell phone, dialed a number, and quietly spoke to someone on the other end.

"The bus will be here in less than half an hour to take us home," he said.

The other guests had also scrambled out of their seats and bolted up the stairs right after Kate and Robbie. They scattered to their assigned rooms, and ten minutes later they were packed and headed out the front door.

"Wait," called Allison, trying to gather the group together. 'You have nowhere to go out there."

Ralph and Greg rounded up the kids and took a head count. Everyone was there and everyone was prepared to leave.

"Now let's quietly move out of the house and down to the end of the driveway," suggested Greg calmly. "I have transportation coming and we'll wait there. The rain has stopped and the moon gives enough light to see our way."

The group, relieved that someone was making the decisions, followed his instructions, accompanied by Allison and her brother. Mrs. Beale stood on the steps wringing her hands.

"I'm so sorry," she said. "Nothing like this has ever happened before."

"Mrs. Beale," said Greg, "If this was not a parlor trick…if this is real…you are in danger also. You need to come with us."

"I'll be fine. This is my home. I can't leave it just yet. Somehow I'll find a way to stop him." She sounded desperate and not at all like the cool, confident woman who guided them into the library for the séance.

"Greg, this has to be some kind of scam. There's no such thing as ghosts…" protested Miranda.

"Oh, child, you have a lot to learn," said Mrs. Beale shakily. "This is no scam."

"No," agreed Greg, "I don't believe it is. I work for SIUP, the Society for Investigation of Unexplained Phenomenon. The Society has been watching this house and recording events here since the late 60's when the first death occurred. Neither we nor the police have ever been able to explain some of the events or any of the murders. They had no suspects, no motive, no murder weapon. Robert Bennett was indeed the first victim. We also count all the interim owners who met their death under mysterious circumstances.

"Now we know that the murderer is no longer available to catch. Apparently, according to Robert Bennett, the house is the next victim. We all need to be gone when that happens."

"How did you get a bus to come so quickly?" inquired Miranda, suddenly realizing that no one expected to pick them up till the next evening.

"I had one on standby. Just had a feeling this weekend wasn't going to be one of those non-eventful kind of trips. The Society's bus was available whenever I called. Now let's get down to the end of the driveway with the rest of the group. Mrs. Beale, please come with us,"

"Thank you, but no. I have a lot of things to pack if I have to leave. I have a van in the garage out back, but I can't leave just yet. I have to try to talk him out of destroying the house.'"

"You sound like you know the murderer. Do you?" asked Miranda, curiously.

"My husband," admitted the lady with a sigh. "He passed away last year. Adam was a very evil man. He also had a very powerful mind. He could do things with his thoughts that you would not believe. I've suspected what he had been doing for years, but I couldn't stop him. He would never listen to me. Now I just have to try to talk him out of whatever he is planning. It's over; it just has to be over."

Greg took Miranda's arm and they hurried down the driveway where the bus had already pulled up and was loading its passengers. A few minutes later the driver made a hasty U-turn and started down the road, the group excitedly chattering and some of the girls shaking and sobbing a bit.

Suddenly there was a tremendous blast. They looked back and saw a ball of fire where the house stood. A second explosion shot flames up into the air and turned the building into a raging inferno. Everyone became very quiet.

"Poor Mrs. Beale," whispered Miranda. "I guess he wouldn't listen to her this time either."

"Now it really is over," said Greg. "The Society believes that the house was the link. The first three deaths, considered murders, took place there. All three of the new owners that planned to renovate or tear down the house died under mysterious circumstances, and all had spent at least one night in the house. With the house burned to the ground, the doorway is closed."

He had the rapt attention of everyone as they gathered around to hear the story while the bus rumbled down the highway.

"What about the present owner?" Kate asked.

"He lives overseas and has never been inside the house." Greg replied. "He bought it because of its reputation and decided to turn it into a weekend haunted excursion retreat."

"When did the Beales become involved?" asked Allison.

"Mrs. Beale and her husband moved in shortly before the first death. They acted as housekeeper and groundskeeper. No one suspected him since he had no motive and the manner in which each man died was so bizarre. After the third death, they stayed on as caretakers but the house simply remained on the market for two decades. No one wanted a house that had been the scene of three mysterious deaths, whether or not they were murders."

"What do you mean by bizarre? How did they all die?" asked one of the boys.

"Robert Bennett, the first victim, apparently choked to death. There was no sign of foul play and he always locked his bedroom door at night. His family could hear him choking and had to break the door down to get to him, but it was too late. The marks on his neck seemed to indicate that he had been strangled, but there was no one in the room and no murder weapon.

"The second victim was his brother, who was found in the cellar two months later, apparently scared to death. They claimed the look on his face was of complete terror and his heart stopped from fear. The third jumped, fell or was pushed from the turret less than three months later. No one was home at the time. The Beales were in town shopping, the victim's wife was visiting her sister and his children were at school. He had no known reason to commit suicide and left no note behind, so the official ruling was accidental, but in view of the other two deaths, no one believed it."

"So everybody was afraid of living in the house," ventured Ralph thoughtfully. "I read an article about Hawley House several years ago. It reported mysterious noises and lights and officially declared the house as haunted. It was on the market for years."

Greg nodded, and continued, "Finally someone bought the house, spent one night there and died in a boating accident the following week. The second owner also spent a night there and was killed when his car was hit by a bus on his way back to the city. Number three, who managed to get electricity installed, had a heart attack in his own home two months after he started the renovations…he was only thirty-two and had no previous heart condition. He visited the house just once to see how the installation was coming and died a few days later.

"Adam Beale died just before the last time the house was sold. The new owner is one of our Society members and knows the history of the house. Mrs. Beale was allowed to stay because she couldn't leave. She would have died if she had tried, and she and the owner both knew it."

Kate peered over the back of the seat at Miranda. "What do you say we don't tell Mom about this?" she suggested. "We'll have to stay at a motel tonight or she'll wonder why we're home so early."

"Greg says there's a motel down the road from the Society where we can get a room, and he'll drive us home tomorrow afternoon after lunch. I totally agree. This is nothing we want to have to explain to Mother. Let's just say we had an interesting weekend."

"And met a couple of really nice guys," Kate laughed, and added with a 'tongue-in-cheek' smirk. "That should make her very happy."

They grinned at each other. Miranda rolled her eyes, envisioning the scene that would happen if their control freak mother thought either of her daughters was interested in any particular man.

Kate is growing up, thought Miranda. Despite the hair-raising experience, she was very glad she came. This weekend certainly changed her relationship with her sister for the better! If they stick together, they should be able to break their mother's control over their lives. Things were about to change drastically in their household. Miranda was going to start dating Greg, and Kate was obviously intending to spend time with Robbie. Mother would just have to get used to the idea and accept it.

Miranda isn't as stuffy as I thought she was, reflected Kate. Having a big sister to hang out with is rather nice, after all. Maybe Robbie and I can double date with Miranda and Greg…wouldn't that be a trip! And maybe life at home won't be so bad with an ally in the house!

With any luck, Greg would be able to keep the story out of the media, and their mother would never know about the fire or what happened at Hawley House that weekend.

With A Little Help

It really wasn't any darker than it would have been at 6 or 7 o'clock, Shelly told herself. No reason to panic. The streets of Manning were probably as safe as anywhere…even safer. It was the dead of winter, and close to zero. The only sound she could hear was the crunch of her boots on the snow. She wrapped her scarf even tighter around her face, put her head down and trudged resolutely on.

She wasn't cold. She was too angry to be cold. Bobby Edwards had some nerve! She should have known there was a catch when he offered to drive her home. She would have been better off waiting at the bus stop like she planned, but he had never given her any indication that he was "that kind" of guy. Actually, she had rather liked him. He was friendly, pleasant and respectful to her at work. She heard other girls in the office talking about him and his "hands on" approach, but she didn't take it seriously. After all, he never had made a move on her or even so much as flirted, so he obviously wasn't attracted to her.

It never occurred to her that he would drive down the first dark lane, stop the car and try to kiss her…if that's what you could call it. The man must have six hands, she thought ruefully. And all she had expected was to be driven home quickly in a nice warm car after working till 10 o'clock at night on a project for the office.

What was even more despicable was when she got out of the car and started walking… he let her! He simply started the car and drove off down the road in the other direction, leaving her alone on the deserted street at night. What kind of man would do that? She briefly considered filing sexual harassment charges against him but gave up that idea almost immediately. Bobby was the owner's brother-in-law and if came to a choice, she would undoubtedly be the one to go.

Up ahead a car was parked by the side of the road under the streetlight. She could see two men leaning up against the car, watching her approach. Her heart pounding, she could actually taste her fear, but she had no other direction to go. Her apartment was two blocks on the other side of that car and was her destination.

Suddenly, the two men jumped into the car and sped off. She let out her breath in a sigh of relief. She had just imagined the threat. Then she heard a sound behind her and quickly looked back. She was being followed by a huge white dog. He wagged his tail when she saw him and she knew he was friendly. Apparently the two men down the road didn't know that, however, and now she knew why they had left so quickly.

"Are you protecting me, boy?" she asked, and the dog wagged his tail even harder. "Are you lost? I wish I could take you home with me, but there's no room in my little apartment for a dog your size."

By now he was trotting along beside her and didn't seem the least concerned where they were going. He was so big she could reach over and scratch his ears without even leaning over. His company comforted her, and when they reached her apartment, she fumbled in her bag for her key and then turned to speak to the dog. However, he was nowhere in sight. He had just simply vanished.

Taking a deep breath, Shelly let herself into the apartment and locked the door behind her. She would never get used to those episodes, even though strange things had been happening to her all her life.

When she was six, she tried to take a shortcut through a wooded area to get home faster, even though her mother had always warned her about leaving the street. Although it was not a big area, Shelly at six was not a very big girl, and she soon realized she was lost. She had no way of telling which way was out. She was about to burst into tears when a huge tabby cat wandered up to her, rubbed herself on Shelly's leg and then proceeded to head down the path, turning to look at Shelly and letting out a commanding meow. Shelly had a feeling she should follow the cat even though it appeared to be heading deeper into the woods. So she did, and within a few minutes, she found herself back on the street below her house, and the cat had simply vanished.

At age thirteen, Shelly fell off her bike down by the lake when she was camping with her parents, spraining her ankle. She couldn't walk, there was a storm brewing and everyone had deserted the beach. She was scared, but was soon found by the storekeeper, who told her that her dog, a big black lab, had barked and barked at him and kept running toward the lake and then coming back and barking some more. The storekeeper finally followed the dog, deciding that something must be wrong. He found Shelly, but the dog had disappeared. No one at the lake owned such a dog or ever remembered seeing a big black lab.

There were other such incidents, too. The bird that kept dive bombing her until she turned back, and then she discovered a rattler had been lying on the path that she would have surely stepped on if she had kept going. The ringing telephone that woke her up late one night, just in time to stop a potential fire. She had accidentally left the burner on and the pan was hot and beginning to smolder. Her caller ID indicated that there had been no call at that time.

She had long since stopped trying to figure them out, never told anyone about them, and just accepted the help when it came from whatever source. Too bad her helpers hadn't warned her about Bobby Edwards before she accepted the ride.

Because they had worked late the night before, the office manager announced that they would be closing at noon. Amanda was fine with that, since she still had some Christmas shopping to do and packages to send. Apparently she wasn't going to spend the holidays with her parents and siblings in Florida. She tried…calling the airlines three different times. The first time she was disconnected. The second time she got a reservation clerk that literally couldn't speak English. The woman translated Florida into Florence, and Amanda simply hung up, not wishing to spend her holiday in Italy. The third time she kept getting wrong numbers. She sighed, took that as a sign that she wasn't supposed to go, and resigned herself to sending the gifts by FedEx overnight.

The next morning when she arrived at work, the secretaries were giggling in the corner. Normally Shelly didn't involve herself in office gossip, but Nancy called her over and said, "Did you hear what happened to Bobby Edwards? His car broke down last night on Old Plank Road--just quit on him, and he had to walk in the freezing cold six miles for help with no boots and no coat -only his suit jacket."

Bobby was, to say the least, very vain. He was always dressed in an expensive suit and tie to give the impression that he was an important businessman. He never saw the need to wear a coat, since he was going from a heated office to a heated car parked in a heated garage under the building, and then home to another heated garage. Well, well, well. Her guardians were apparently taking care of that situation, too. She didn't think she'd have any more trouble with Bobby. Indeed, when they passed in the hall, he mumbled something that sounded like 'gud mor-dig' followed by a hefty sneeze and quickly scooted into his office.

Shelly, while grateful for the help each time, felt somewhat like a freak. She rarely dated...what man would understand the strange episodes? She never told her parents...they would have immediately sought psychiatric help for her, both being in the scientific field and not open to anything that couldn't be explained medically or scientifically.

As a child, she thought everyone had "helpers"... that it was just a normal part of life. She couldn't understand why bad things happened to people, especially kids. Where were their helpers? As she grew older, she realized that her situation was different. She tried telling her best friend about it once, but the girl just looked at her like she had lost her mind, and from that day forward, avoided any contact with her. So Shelly became withdrawn. She avoided office parties, lunches with the girls, and had the reputation of being rather aloof, while inside she was very lonely and felt cursed rather than blessed with being unique. She was outwardly friendly to everyone, but very cautious about close friendships. And even the ones she associated with at work didn't know about her "curse."

"Hey, Mandy. Wait up." Candy was running down the hall to the elevator. Candy was one of Amanda's few friends at the office. The two of them made an unusual pair. Candy was very short and slightly overweight, with a round face, short black curly hair and brown eyes. Amanda was almost the opposite, tall, thin, long blonde hair and blue eyes.

"If you want to come shopping with me, I have the car today," Candy offered, punching the button for the bottom floor.

"Thanks. That'd be great!"

"Thought you were going to Florida for Christmas."

"Changed my mind," said Amanda. Of course, Candy didn't know about the "episodes" and she would just think it was silly that Amanda, based on three problems with phone calls, was going to miss Christmas with her family. Actually, Candy would probably be right. Maybe she should just ignore these "signs" and make her reservations anyway.

She found the perfect scarf for her mother and a Star Wars toy for her ten-year-old nephew and she was finished. They had a quick bite to eat at a bistro in the mall and then Candy dropped her at her apartment. As she wrapped the rest of the gifts to mail, she decided she would try once more to make reservations, picked up the phone and found it disconnected…dead…no dial tone. "Okay," she said out loud. "I get the message…again."

At 6 am on Christmas Eve morning, she woke up and then turned over and went back to sleep. She wasn't catching the plane, so no need to drag out of bed at that ungodly hour. She was having Christmas dinner with Candy and her family but she had no plans for Christmas Eve. Maybe she would walk over to St Claire's church and attend mass that evening. Maybe she would catch a cab to the theater and see a movie. Maybe…she would just stay home and feel sorry for herself.

When she woke up at nine, she turned on the TV in time to catch the announcement that the plane she had been going to catch had gone down in Pennsylvania while trying to land. The landing gear had never descended, unbeknownst to the pilot. Of the ninety passengers aboard, over half of them were injured at least slightly and several more severely. All were stranded and probably wouldn't arrive at their destination until Christmas Day. So this was why she wasn't able to make reservations! Maybe that movie sounded good after all. She mentally thanked her helpers, suddenly very hungry, and headed to the kitchen to make breakfast.

As she grew older, unexpected intervention wasn't the only thing she experienced. Sometimes she knew things about people…knew what was going to happen or what they were doing that they hid from the world. These things she tried to ignore. When one of the men in the office came in on crutches, claiming he sprained his ankle on the ski slope, she just grinned to herself, knowing full well he hurt himself when he fell down the stairs while drunk over the weekend. She overheard Gloria telling the other girls that her boyfriend was cheating on her and she threw him out. However, she knew that the man left because he caught Gloria in a compromising situation with his best friend.

It was slow the week between Christmas and New Years. Several people were out on vacation and there really wasn't much to do, but as she passed one of her co-workers, she suddenly knew he was headed for a serious accident on the way home. Should she tell him? Maybe there was another way.

"Jeff, I need a favor."

Jeff looked up in surprise. For as many years as they had been working together, Shelly had never asked him for anything.

"Sure…how can I help you?"

"I'm having a little problem with the quarterly financial report. Would you mind staying a few minutes after work and helping me check the figures on the spreadsheet? It shouldn't take more than half an hour, if that, and I would really appreciate it."

"No problem. Glad to help."

She made a few quick changes in the figures on the report to give him something to find. Jeff stopped by after work and they went over the sheets together, and her "errors" were found in about 20 minutes. Shelly thanked him profusely, intuitively feeling that he had missed the time for the accident.

The next morning, Jeff stopped by her desk.

"I want to thank you for asking me to help you yesterday. Do you know there was a seven-car pileup on the freeway? If I had left at my usual time, I would have been right in the middle of it. They were just starting to clear it up when I reached that point last night. Guess I was just really lucky, huh!"

"Really lucky," smiled Shelly. "Thanks for helping me with the report."

One morning the CEO called her into the office and asked her to shut the door. With a sick feeling in her stomach, Shelly did as she was asked.

"We have a problem, Shelly," he began. "I've noticed that you seem to be more…observant that most of my staff, and I am asking for your help in solving it."

"What's the problem, sir?" she asked, somehow knowing that this was going to be a life-changing moment.

"Embezzlement," he said bluntly. "I could dress it up with another term, but the bottom line is…someone is stealing from the company. I have a suspicion I know who, but until I can prove it, my hands are tied. You seem to have a handle on what goes on around here and all I'm asking is for you to just be as …observant as you usually are and focus on solving the problem."

"I'll do my best, Mr. Johnson, but I'm not sure how much help I…"

"I'm putting you in charge of Accounts Receivable. This will give you the authority and access to records you wouldn't otherwise have. I don't expect miracles, you understand, but I have a feeling you are the best person for this assignment here."

As their eyes met, Shelly suddenly was sure that Mr. Johnson knew her secret… knew how she obtained information no one else had.

"When…when do I start?" she asked shakily.

He smiled. "Right now," he said. "The memo to the staff is going out as we speak."

"You do the same thing I do, don't you?" she blurted out.

"Almost, but I'm not quite as good at it. And in this case, I'm not in…shall we say…the position to obtain the actual evidence without raising suspicion, as you will be as Accounts Receivable Manager.

Remember, we need hard evidence, so even when you know who it is… and I'm sure you will very shortly…we need physical proof."

"You'll have it, Mr. Johnson, as quickly as I can get it for you."

"By the way, since you'll be in upper management now, we go by first names. I'm Frank."

He smiled again as he walked her to the door. "Just go right down to Personnel and they will take care of having you sign the promotion paperwork. It should be ready by now. Welcome aboard, Shelly."

So she wasn't the only one. Just that fact alone almost had her walking on air. She wasn't a one-of-a-kind freak. Other people had the same gift, and she was willing to bet that she and Frank Johnson were only two out of hundreds, maybe thousands.

With suppressed excitement, she took the elevator to the floor below to the Personnel office where the clerk shoved papers across the counter for her signature. A few scribbles and she was promoted to Accounts Receivable Manager, with a hefty pay raise, an office to herself with her name on the door, and an assignment.

By the next day, news of her promotion had spread like wildfire. Some offered congratulations, some were jealous and some were openly resentful. The previous AR Manager had, a few weeks before, decided to retire, and the resentful ones thought they should have been considered for the position.

It only took a couple of weeks for Shelly to come up to speed on the responsibilities of the job. She had already had some experience, having taken on some of the duties when the AR Manager went on vacation. Frank stopped in occasionally to see if she had any questions, and she usually did, but she grasped the entire scope of the job much faster than she had expected.

One quiet morning she sat at her desk, closed her eyes and concentrated on the word "embezzlement." She received several impressions which were confusing at first. She saw a big clock, a plate of oysters and a pile of sparkly stones that appeared to be diamonds. These items rotated in and out of windows, and it didn't make much sense to her.

Her impressions did direct her to the merchandise from the three jewelry stores, however. She checked inventory lists, all of which seemed to be fine. Any items missing from inventory were accounted for by sales. On the surface, everything appeared normal, but something kept telling her to look deeper.

The first odd thing she noticed was an inordinate amount of activity on certain items…high end items…starting approximately two months ago. All of the items were fairly small, and all were expensive.

Based on her impressions of a big clock…time…she picked the most expensive man's watch to track. According to the return records, it had been purchased at Store #1 in Hillside for cash and returned there the same day for a full refund. The same brand of man's watch was returned to the store for refund five times over the next two weeks. One might surmise that there was a problem with the watch…perhaps a manufacturing defect. However, Store #2 in Breaton had no returns of that watch and, Store #3 in Chester showed no returns, either.

A closer scrutiny of the records showed that this was not the only item that generated a similar scenario. Although the watch was not a problem at the other stores, there was a rather expensive diamond necklace that retailed for $2500 returned to Breaton three times and a string of pearls for $1200 that generated returns in Chester. This was all within the last two months. While a watch might have a manufacturing defect, it was unlikely that several diamond necklaces and strings of pearls were returned for the same reason. It seemed that each store's multiple returns focused on only one specific item, and never during the same period.

Inventories balanced, showing that the items were, in fact, not missing from the stores, but something about the whole scenario bothered Shelly. Store #1, for instance, had a large number of returned watches totaling almost $3400. Store #2 had returns of the diamond necklace for about $7,500, and Store #3 paid out some $2280 for returned pearls. Just those items alone created a loss of income of over $13,000 between the three stores during the two weeks she picked to track. It was surely a blow to the business, but how could it be embezzlement? She checked the history of each store for returns, but until three months ago, there were very few items being returned… maybe one or two a month, and often it was simply an exchange for a different item rather than a return for cash.

She checked to see which clerks accepted the returns, but there were several different ones at the three stores. She decided maybe she was focusing on the wrong thing and resolved to try another track.

The next morning, she awoke before the alarm went off, which wasn't unusual. She noticed the time was 5:12 am, which was about 45 minutes before she usually woke. Later she stopped for coffee at the convenient store, grabbed a pastry, and paid the bill of $5.12. Driving to work, she became aware that the car ahead of her had an unusual license plate…the number was 512-512. In the office, she updated her desk calendar, tearing off the previous sheet, and realized that the date was….May 12th…another 512. Must be something to do with that number, she thought. Where had she seen that number before?

Suddenly it registered! The man's watch she had tracked was retailing for $512 and 0000512 was the number of the sales receipt for the first purchase of that watch from the store. Excited, she dug out the receipts that she had filed away the day before. Yes, the first receipt number was 0000512. When she began checking the returned slips, every one of them from Store #1 indicated that all eight returned watches over the two-week period had the same receipt number listed on the return slip record! Per company policy, when merchandise is returned, the item is circled in red and initialed on the original sales slip, the receipt number is recorded on a return record, and then the receipt is returned to the buyer. The return records are included in each day's business, so they are never all together in one place. Hard copies of sales and returns are sent to Corporate once a week.

It took most of the morning to check the paper trail for the diamond necklace and the string of pearls to find that the number of the first purchase receipt was the same number posted on every return slip record for that item.

Mystery solved…or at least partially solved. Now all she had to do was check to see who signed the returns. Was it the same person? No, there were several different clerks involved in the three stores. So where did the thieves get the items to return? Just knowing what happened wasn't enough. Frank Johnson wanted proof…so proof she would get him.

She went back to the watch that was the first item purchased from Store #1. Checking the clerk's ID number, she cross matched to her list and wrote down "Marilee Hopkins." Marilee sold the first diamond necklace at Breaton and the first pearl necklace at Chester also.

There was only one department that has the ability to move employees from one store to another. Shelly called the head of Personnel.

"John, I need some information. I notice that you have assigned Marilee Hopkins, employee #42, to three different stores over the past three months. Is this common?"

"We do move people around for a lot of reasons," confirmed John. "I can check and see why we moved Marilee if you like. Hold on."

A few minutes later, he returned to the phone. "That clerk was transferred by order of our illustrious Vice President. Breaton was having some kind of promotion on diamonds and Bobby said this girl was somewhat of an expert, having worked for a jewelry company before she was hired here. He thought she would be an asset during the promotion."

"And why was she sent to Chester?"

"Basically the same reason. Her background in working for a company that specialized in pearls and particularly pearls in the oyster. She had a lot of training and information on cultured pearls. He said they were doing a promotion in Chester for pearls and needed an expert for a few weeks there. She's still in Chester but the promotion is over and she will be returning to Hillside shortly. Is there a problem, Shelly?"

"No, no problem. I was checking on something and her name came up in all three stores. Just curious."

What a mess! If Bobby was involved, there would be a real uproar. Being the brother of the owner's wife made the whole situation very sensitive. She would have to be very careful about accusing anyone of anything before having all the facts.

Frank had to be told, she thought, and headed upstairs to his office.

He motioned her to come in, and she shut the door behind her.

"First of all," she began, sliding a spreadsheet and flow chart across the desk to him, "the system you are using leaves much to be desired. I'm surprised there haven't been more incidents like this. It is almost impossible to find errors and omissions, even honest mistakes, unless you know exactly what you are looking for."

Frank nodded. "I know our computer system isn't the best…"

"Actually, it isn't the computer, it's the accounting system. Stores report sales on a daily basis and we download the information, but the income is only separated by credit sales and cash sales. There is no backup information to determine what was sold. Returned items are posted on a return record, but that is kept in the stores and only turned in once a week with hard copies of the sales receipts for that week. Cash returns are simply deducted from the cash sales for whatever day the return is made. How did you ever decide there was a problem with embezzlement?"

Frank simply raised his eyebrows, and Shelly had to laugh. Of course she knew how he knew, but she was not used to other people having her "special talent."

"I think I can tell you where the money is going," she said, pointing to the flow chart. "This is what is going on. A customer purchases an item, a man's watch, and pays $512 plus tax in cash. The item is returned, usually the same day, and a refund given. However, there is a 5% restocking fee, so the customer only receives $486.40 plus the tax back. A photocopy has already been made of the receipt--several photocopies, in fact. The customer then steals four more watches, with the help of the clerk who waits until just after the semimonthly inventory has been done. The customer uses the photocopies--which are excellent duplicates--to return the watches-- to the same store but not to the same clerk. This explains why the inventory doesn't show any shortage. Items that are stolen are being returned to the store … for a cash refund… and put back in stock before the next inventory."

"Clever," said Frank. "But why hasn't anyone caught this before? Somewhere there should be a very definite paper trail with the name of the customer and clerk. Which store is this happening at?"

"Actually, it's all three stores, and for different pieces of jewelry at each store. It isn't likely that three different clerks would be involved. And they aren't. In fact, there is only one, and that clerk has been transferred to the different stores on a periodic basis. The person in question is Marilee Hopkins. I believe she is the one who is furnishing the items from each store to be returned when she is not there, so her name isn't showing up on all the return slips."

"How much jewelry are we talking here?"

"There are three items involved in this scheme. The man's watch retailing for $512, a diamond necklace for $2500 and a string of pearls for $1200. The same procedure was used for each one and each one is from a different store."

"We do get hard copies of the transactions from the stores, so why hasn't anyone caught this before?" Frank frowned, studying the flow chart.

"As I said, returns are only reported once a week. Apparently no one has ever compared the returns to the sales receipts. This would be difficult anyway, since our policy allows a return within 30 days so the sale could have been made anytime during the past month. The stolen items, with the photocopied receipts, are actually returned to the store prior to the next inventory, so the balances won't be short at the next count to alert anyone to a problem. "

"So you're saying that whoever is doing this is very familiar with our record keeping system?"

"Absolutely. We generally only look at each thing separately. If the item was purchased for cash, the return items are reimbursed in cash for the retail cost plus tax minus the 5% restocking fee. The fact that we charge a restocking fee further makes it difficult to pinpoint missing funds. The receipt for purchase that is brought in with the item looks legitimate and only the receipt number is recorded on the return record, with the actual receipt – the photocopy, that is - circled in red and returned to the customer. The next item brought in has a fresh photocopy with it, of course. Since the return is to different clerks over a period of time, there is no reason to connect the purchase receipt number to the last return."

"So do we have enough evidence to have this Marilee arrested?" asked Frank.

"Right now it's just circumstantial. I can give you copies of all the paperwork, but it won't prove she is the one involved. Now the real culprit here is her partner… and I must tell you that here is where we may run into a problem. She was assigned to each of the stores during the exact times the scams took place, and the person responsible for having her sent to the different stores… is Bobby Edwards, our owner's brother-in-law. I don't know how you want to handle this."

Frank sighed. "I suspected as much," he admitted. "How much is the damage?"

"Over $35,000 during the past two months. Apparently, this started shortly before George retired, so nothing would have shown up until after he was gone."

"Keep this under your hat for the time being, Shelly. We need some really hard evidence before I present it to the old man. He isn't going to be a happy camper. I think we're going to have to actually nail the person is that is returning the stolen items to the store."

"You know, I don't think that will be a problem for much longer. I have a feeling that they are going to push their luck at the Chester store before Marilee is reassigned back to Hillside. They are scheduled to do the regular semimonthly audit at Chester tonight, so this is the ideal time for another hit. It's just a matter of which piece of jewelry it will be. There are so many high-end pieces to choose from."

"Do the best you can, Shelly. I'm sure we'll have our answer soon."

Shelly wasn't sure exactly what the next step would be. How would she know which piece they would tag as their next scam? Maybe she should just rely on her "special talent" to point the way. Back in her office, she said aloud, "OK, friends. Now is when I need your help. We have to catch these thieves, and I'm relying on you to give me the information I need."

Things were quiet over the weekend. Monday morning Shelly stopped for her usual morning coffee and was drawn to a magazine she had not noticed before. Its name was Emerald Isle. The name seemed to jump right out at her, and she nodded, took her coffee and stood in line to pay. OK. There was a clue…maybe. Emeralds. The stores did sell emeralds, some of which were very exquisite pieces.

The lady ahead of her seemed to be having a problem, and the clerk and the rest of the customers were becoming impatient. She was digging in her purse and counting out change to pay for her purchases. Finally, she announced in triumph, "There! I have it all. Eighteen Dollars and Eighty-Eight cents!" There was an audible sigh from the customers behind Shelly, but Shelly wasn't paying attention to the delay. She was paying attention to the numbers just announced…eighteen dollars and eighty-eight cents. She could hardly wait to get to the office.

As soon as she dropped her purse on the desk and sat her coffee on the corner, she grabbed the inventory manual and began flipping the pages. When she came to the listing of emerald pieces, she ran her finger down the retail column until she came to the number she was looking for…$1888.00. It was a gorgeous emerald necklace. There were only five sent to the Chester store, and a quick check of the receipts for Chester for Saturday located a cash sale for the exact amount that was most likely the emerald necklace. Assuming it was, that would leave four more available.

She headed upstairs to Frank Johnson's office.

"Frank, what time does the Chester store close tonight?"

"Five, I think. Why?"

Can you get me into the store after hours? I know what piece will be the next one. If we can prove there are less than four necklaces in stock right now…as inventory indicates…all we have to do is lay a trap for the person who will be bringing them back to return them. I believe the first one has already been sold and will be returned today or tomorrow, if it hasn't been already. That means the receipt has already been copied and the other pieces are already gone. This is our only chance to catch our thieves red-handed…or green handed in this case."

"I'll call Sam, the manager at Chester and have him meet us at six to let us in. If you don't mind, we can leave right from the office and I'll drive."

The conversation on the short twenty-minute trip was very interesting. Shelly wanted to know more about Frank's "special talent" and gave him some interesting tales about her own experiences. It was refreshing to talk openly to someone who understood and empathized with the problems of being "different." Frank was fortunate in that his parents were both into metaphysical studies and they encouraged him to use his intuition. She was almost sorry when they reached their destination and had to cut their conversation off, although Frank promised they would have many more occasions to talk in the future.

Sam was waiting for them in front of the store. He took them back to the safe where the jewelry was kept, grabbing the inventory book on the way. It didn't take long to discover that the inventory record showed five emerald necklaces in stock, the one sold having been returned that morning, but there were only three in the safe. It was a safe bet that over the next two weeks, the two missing necklaces would be back in the safe, having been returned for a cash refund. Someone would collect close to $3600—not bad for a few day's work.

Frank asked Sam about his clerks for the jewelry counter and was told that, outside of Marilee who had returned to Hillside that afternoon, he had four salesclerks. One was his daughter and one his godson and the other two had been with him for several years. He assured Frank and Shelly that he trusted all four implicitly. Sam agreed to alert his clerks to call Shelly or Frank at the corporate office if anyone brought in an emerald necklace with a cash receipt for a return. Marilee had already signed the return slip for the first necklace that had been legitimately purchased for cash, so any future returns were sure to be part of the stolen merchandise.

Now there was nothing to do but wait. Two days passed with no call, but at 9:45 a.m. on Thursday, Shelly took a call from Andrea, Sam's daughter. There was a man in the store asking for a refund for an emerald necklace. He claimed he bought it for his wife, who decided she did not like emeralds. She told him that her computer was down and that the manager would have to process his return and called for her father. Then she slipped into the back and called Shelly.

They dropped everything and headed for the car and the store in Chester, hoping that Sam could stall him for the twenty minutes it would take to get there.

When they entered the store, the man, dressed in an expensive suit, was standing at the counter, his back toward the door. Sam was bent over the paperwork taking his time in filling out the record while the man impatiently fidgeted and seemed rather nervous. Frank walked up behind him and tapped him on the shoulder, and Bobby Edwards swung around, shocked.

"Sorry, Bobby. You're busted," said Frank, punching numbers in his cell phone. Bobby spun around and tried to leave, but Sam had security standing by and the two burly guards made sure he stayed put. In a few minutes Frank had the owner on the line. It was up to the Mr. Richards to decide what to do about his brother-in-law, but Shelly wouldn't have given two cents for his chances of avoiding the full fury of Mr. Richards and his wife, Bobby's sister.

A few days later Shelly was called back into Frank's office. She fully expected to be demoted back to her old position, now that the problem was solved.

"Not a chance, Shelly. You accepted the position, and now you're stuck with it," grinned Frank. "We need a major overhaul of our record keeping methods to avoid this in the future. I'm counting on you to put security measures in place that will prevent anyone from circumventing the system again. "

Bobby was, of course, fired, and his sister refused to forgive him, although she did prevail upon her husband not to press charges. Bobby admitted, and in fact couldn't resist bragging, that the whole scheme was his brainstorm. During his short tenure as VP, he had dated one of the accounting clerks for a few weeks. Once he learned how the antiquated system was set up, he hatched the clever scheme.

Then he coerced and blackmailed Marilee Hopkins into helping him, threatening to have her accused of stealing and then fired if she didn't cooperate. Marilee, a single mother, needed every cent of her paycheck to take care of her disabled son, and she was panicked into doing what Bobby wanted. Greedily, he didn't even give her any extra money from his embezzled funds!

Mr. Richards felt sorry for Marilee but obviously couldn't trust her in his stores any longer. His wife, however, helped her find another position at a day care center near Marilee's apartment. Her income would be the same but she had free childcare for her son, plus no transportation costs as she and her son could simply walk down the street. Knowing how manipulative Bobby was and how he had blackmailed the poor woman made Mrs. Richards very compassionate, and she felt it was the least she could do to make up for what her brother had done.

Back in her apartment, Shelly felt her life was just beginning. Frank had promised to introduce her to his friends and family where she could relate to others with similar talents and just be herself. She had a new challenging job and the authority to make changes to the accounting system to bring it up to date. Mr. Richards had been very impressed and more than willing to give her a free hand.

And she still had her "helpers" to give her guidance when she needed it. Life couldn't be any sweeter!

Shelter From the Storm

It was raining. Not just a gentle sprinkle of water, but a full-fledged, roaring, driving force rainstorm complete with thunder and lightning!

Austin had never been so wet or cold in her life. She trudged down the road, feet squishing in her soaking wet boots; head down against the rain that seemed to come at her horizontally. Water ran down her face, down her thick dark hair, down the back of her neck. She was miles away from town, miles away from any civilization at all. Apparently her cell phone didn't work that far out in the country, but she should have stayed with the car which had gone off the road some two miles behind her.

Suddenly a flash of lightning lit up the countryside for a few seconds, and Austin was sure she saw the outline of a building off to her right. It didn't matter if it was a house, or a barn, or just a broken-down shack. It was shelter, and she desperately needed to get to it.

It took her a good fifteen minutes to make her way toward where she remembered the silhouette had been, and when she arrived, she breathed a sigh of relief. It was a house, and it appeared to be empty. Pushing open the back door, she stumbled inside and realized that although it might be empty, it was not deserted. It opened into a cozy kitchen where a vase of flowers sat upon a table that was covered with a bright print cloth. The wood cook stove was throwing off heat and a pot of something which smelled heavenly was simmering on the back.

She kicked off her boots and wet socks and left them on the mat by the back door, then stripped off the soggy coat and scarf and hung them on the hook on the wall by the stove to dry. Her pant legs were wet, but there was nothing she could do about that. She grabbed a dishtowel from the counter to mop some of the rain from her face and hair, and then stood in front of the stove, hands extended to the heat, and said a prayer of thanks that she had found shelter.

After she caught her breath, she called out "Hello, is anyone home?" but there was silence. Barefoot, she padded through the door into the next room. There was a long sofa and end tables, with two lamps that were turned on. Heavy drapes covered the windows, which explained why she had not seen any light from the road. The room was warm and comfortable, although there was no sign of a heater or stove inside. Curious, she opened the door to another room to find a small but charming bedroom. Another door revealed a bathroom and she eyed the shower in the corner longingly. She felt at that moment like she would never be warm again. Perhaps her reluctant host or hostess would allow her to have a hot shower.

She returned to the kitchen. Where on earth was the owner of this haven? No one would go off and leave food cooking on the stove, lights on in the living room and the door unlocked for very long. Perhaps there was a barn she could not see where her benefactor was working… milking the cow, feeding the animals, or whatever. She would just sit at the table and wait and hope she didn't give the owner a fright. She had looked for a phone but saw none. There were probably no phone lines this far out in the country. She hoped when the storm stopped that someone who lived here could give her a ride into town to find a tow truck for her vehicle.

Two hours later Austin opened her eyes. She hadn't meant to fall asleep, but apparently she had, head down on the kitchen table. The clock over the cupboard showed that it was after 6 pm. Still no one had come back to the house. The pot was still simmering and she was tempted to take a bowl of the stew. Wouldn't be polite, of course, but where on earth was everyone?

Her pant legs were nearly dry, which was a good thing. Not so with the coat or scarf, or her boots and socks. It was very dark outside. The storm was still raging, with frequent flashes of lightning. Peering out the window wasn't any help. If there was another building, she couldn't see it.

Austin stood up stiffly and stretched. She went to the living room, then the bedroom and bathroom, looking out all of the windows to see if she could see any sign of life. There was none. Even when the lightning flashes allowed her a view of the surroundings, there didn't appear to be any other building even close to the house. But then there were no windows along the back so she assumed the barn…or whatever other building there was…must be back there out of her sight.

This situation was beginning to make her uncomfortable. She wanted the owner to show up. Houses just didn't sit out in the country like this, with food and a fire waiting, unless there was someone living here. And she had no idea how long no one had been home.

By seven o'clock, Austin's stomach was growling in earnest. Surely the absent owner wouldn't mine if she had a little bowl of the stew. A quick search of the pantry revealed tea bags, sugar, half a loaf of bread and a dish of butter. She cut herself a slice of the bread, then took a bowl from the cupboard and ladled out some of the fragrant cuisine. The teakettle on the counter was filled with water and she set it on the stove to heat for tea.

It tasted even better than it smelled, if that was possible. The bread was fresh, the butter creamy, and the stew in its rich gravy had tender pieces of beef, carrots tomatoes, and some other vegetables she couldn't identify, but they were delicious. The water was soon hot and she made herself a cup of tea, adding a spoonful of sugar. Satisfied, she washed out her bowl and spoon and returned them where they belonged. With nothing else to do, she wandered into the living room with her cup of tea in hand.

Austin sat on the sofa and sipped her tea, but curiosity soon got the better of her. She peeked in the bedroom and then went in and opened the closet door. On the back was a pale blue terrycloth bathrobe. Inside were several flannel shirts and women's jeans. At least she knew her benefactor was female. There was no sign of any men's clothing.

On a shelf inside the bathroom were several fluffy towels, shampoo and conditioner and a bar of soap. It appeared to be a modern bathroom, complete with flushing toilet and the inviting shower Austin had seen earlier. If her hostess didn't return soon, she might just take a chance on that shower.

The living room yielded several books on a bookshelf in the corner. Not having a TV available, she chose one that looked interesting and settled down on the sofa to read while she waited. The storm seemed to be slowing down somewhat, and she was sure the owner would be coming in the door any minute.

Reading always made her sleepy, and her eyes soon drifted shut.. When she next opened them, it was light outside. She realized she was stretched out on the soft and covered with a blanket but couldn't remember pulling the one off the back of the sofa over herself during the night. Perhaps the owner had returned, was kind enough to let her sleep and put the blanket over her. She peeked in the bedroom but nothing had been disturbed. Birds singing outside told her that the storm was over and that it was morning.

When she entered the kitchen, she found her coat and scarf, as well as her boots and socks, a little stiff but dry. The stove was still burning. Good thing, because she knew absolutely nothing about wood stoves and there didn't seem to be a supply of fuel for it nearby. She felt guilty about not putting the stew away the night before. However, it did not seem to have burned dry and looked as tasty as it had been. Another slice of bread and butter, and a chunk of cheese she had missed seeing the night before, added to her breakfast bowl of stew.

Again she made a tour of the windows opening on three sides of the house and confirmed that there were absolutely no other buildings in sight even in daylight. Now she was really worried about the owner.

"Where on earth could a lone woman have gone in that storm? Is she lying in a ditch somewhere out there?" she wondered aloud.

Austin gave into temptation and took a quick hot shower. She started to wonder about all the modern conveniences in the house, but then assumed that there must be a generator somewhere, a septic tank and a hot water heater. She shampooed her hair, used a little of the conditioner and felt almost human again.

By nine o'clock in the morning, Austin had to assume that the owner was not going to be back soon. She had washed her dishes and put the stew away in the little refrigerator, cleaned up the bathroom and hung the towel to dry. Then she shrugged herself into her coat and put on the stiff dry socks and boots.

She wrote a note of explanation to the owner, left it with a twenty-dollar bill on the table under her teacup to pay for the food, and left the house.

The rain had washed everything clean but there were little streams of water all around. She had to concentrate to avoid stepping in a deep puddle as she made her way out toward where she believed was the main road. When she stopped to rest, she turned to look back at the house. In the light of day, she could see that it was all by itself…no barn, no outbuildings…nowhere the absent hostess could have spent the night. Well, there was nothing she could do now. When she got to town, she would notify the police or somebody who could come out and check on the lady.

It was slow going picking her way down the muddy track and it took Austin longer than she expected to find the country road where she had been stranded, and another twenty minutes of hiking to find her car, still stuck in the ditch.

"Guess I better start walking," she muttered. She remembered that she had passed through a town shortly before her car slid into the ditch, so she continued walking in that direction. Except for the patches of mud, it was a rather pleasant hike, but it was over an hour before she sighted what she thought of as "civilization."

At the gas station at the end of town, she was able to arrange for a tow truck for her car.

"Whatcha' doin' down that road?" asked the owner, chewing on the stub of a cigar.

"I thought that was a shortcut to Barrington," Austin replied.

The man laughed. "Nope. Road to Barrington is another four miles down the highway. Turned too soon. No shortcut there. It's a dead-end road. County doesn't keep that one up…no reason to. I'll git your car and tow it into town for ya."

A little further into town she came across the sheriff's office.

"Sir, I think there's a lady that may need some help," Austin began.

"Now just who might that be?" asked the sheriff. He was leaning back in his chair, feet on his desk, and didn't even stand up when she came in.

"I don't know. I was stranded on the road last night in the storm. I came upon a house where I found shelter, but there was no one home."

"And what makes you think anyone needs help? There's several old empty houses around these parts."

"Because there was a fire in the stove, food cooking and lights on, but nobody was there and nobody came in while I was there…all night."

The sheriff put his feet back on the floor. "Well, now," he asked, "exactly where is this house you stayed in?"

"County Road 72, I think it's called."

He sat up straight in the chair. "72, you say? That's a dead end. Nobody lives on that road."

"Well, you're mistaken. Somebody obviously does. It's an adorable house, but there were no outbuildings of any kind. Oh, it was definitely occupied."

"Not since old Mrs. Burton died some five years ago. The place was falling down, last time I saw it."

"Then who lit the wood stove, put the stew on to cook and turned on the lights?" Austin asked. There was a funny feeling starting in the pit of her stomach, and she didn't like it.

"Ain't never been any electricity out that far anyways. Just an old two room shack and an outhouse."

"We must be talking about two different places," Austin said with a relieved sigh.

"Nope. Only house ever been on that road. Come on. I'll take you out there myself so you can see. You show me where this house is that you stayed in, if it ain't the Burton place." The sheriff grabbed a set of keys and escorted her out to a dusty patrol car parked in front of his office.

On the way out of town, they passed the garage owner bringing in Austin's car. "At least I know we're on the right road," muttered Austin.

Several minutes later the sheriff pulled down a rutted old path and stopped in front of a rundown shack. "This it?" he asked.

Austin stared out the window. "No, this isn't it. It must be further down the road."

"Lady, there ain't no 'further down the road.' This is as far as it goes. About thirty yards down there it simply ends in a draw. That's a big ditch to you city folk. You wanna go in and make sure this ain't where you were?"

Austin jumped out of the car and strode purposefully to the door. She opened it and stepped into the kitchen. There was the wood stove, cold and rusty. There was the kitchen table she remembered, but the tablecloth was old and faded.

And there, under a freshly washed teacup, was her note and a twenty-dollar bill.

www.ingramcontent.com/pod-product-compliance
Lightning Source LLC
Chambersburg PA
CBHW031157010826
48971CB00012B/754